W9-DES-289

POISON and Peril

Forensic Toxicology

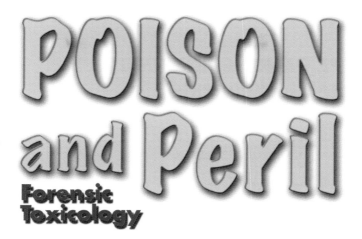

BACON ACADEMY LMC

THE CRIME SCENE CLUB: FACT AND FICTION

THE CRIME SCENE CLUB: FACT AND FICTION

POISON and Peril
Forensic Toxicology

Kenneth McIntosh

Mason Crest Publishers

Poison and Peril: Forensic Toxicology

MASON CREST PUBLISHERS INC.
370 Reed Road
Broomall, Pennsylvania 19008
(866)MCP-BOOK (toll free)
www.masoncrest.com

First Printing

9 8 7 6 5 4 3 2 1

ISBN 978-1-4222-0259-3 (series)
Library of Congress Cataloging-in-Publication Data

McIntosh, Kenneth, 1959–
Poison and peril : forensic toxicology / by Kenneth McIntosh.
    p. cm. — (Crime Scene Club ; case #4)
 Summary: Using the new forensics lab at their Flagstaff charter school, Jessa and the other members of the Crime Scene Club investigate the suspicious death of a local artist.
 Includes bibliographical references (p.).
 ISBN 978-1-4222-0250-0   ISBN 978-1-4222-1453-4
[1. Criminal investigation—Fiction. 2. Forensic sciences—Fiction. 3. Poisons—Fiction. 4. Mystery and detective stories. 5. Flagstaff (Ariz)—Fiction.] I. Title.
PZ7.M1858Po 2009
[Fic]—dc22
                         2008023319

Design by MK Bassett-Harvey.
Produced by Harding House Publishing Service, Inc.
www.hardinghousepages.com
Cover design by MK Bassett-Harvey.
Cover and interior illustrations by Justin Miller.
Printed in Malaysia.

CONTENTS

INTRODUCTION

The sound of breaking glass. A scream. A shot. Then . . . silence. Blood, fingerprints, a bullet, a skull, fire debris, a hair, shoeprints—enter the wonderful world of forensic science. A world of searching to find clues, collecting that which others cannot see, testing to find answers to seemingly impossible questions, and testifying to juries so that justice will be served. A world where curiosity, love of a puzzle, and gathering information are basic. The books in this series will take you to this world.

The CSI Effect

The TV show *CSI: Crime Scene Investigator* became so widely popular that *CSI: Miami* and *CSI: NY* followed. This forensic interest spilled over into *Bones* (anthropology); *Crossing Jordan* and *Dr. G* (medical examiners); *New Detectives* and *Forensic Files*, which cover all the forensic disciplines. Almost every modern detective story now involves forensic science. Many fiction books are written, some by forensic scientists such as Kathy Reichs (anthropology) and Ken Goddard (criminalistics and crime scene), as well as textbooks such as *Criminalistics* by Richard Saferstein. Other crime fiction authors are Sir Arthur Conan Doyle (Sherlock Holmes), Thomas Harris (*Red Dragon*), Agatha Christie (Hercule Poirot) and Ellis Peters, whose hero is a monk, Cadfael, an ex-Crusader who solves crimes. The list goes on and on—and I encourage you to read them all!

The spotlight on forensic science has had good *and* bad effects, however. Because the books and TV shows are so enjoyable, the limits of science have been blurred to make the plots more interesting. Often when students are intrigued by the TV shows and want to learn more, they have a rude awakening. The crime scene investigators on TV do the work of many professionals, including police officers, medical examiners, forensic laboratory scientists, anthropologists, and entomologists, to mention just a few. And all this in addition to processing crime scenes! Fictional instruments give test results at warp speed, and crimes are solved in forty-two minutes. Because of the overwhelming popularity of these shows, juries now expect forensic evidence in every case.

The books in this series will take you to both old and new forensic sciences, perhaps tweaking your interest in a career. If so, take courses in chemistry, biology, math, English, public speaking, and drama. Get a summer job in a forensic laboratory, courthouse, law enforcement agency, or an archeological dig. Seek internships and summer jobs (even unpaid). Skills in microscopy, instrumentation, and logical thinking will help you. Curiosity is a definite plus. You must read and understand procedures; take good notes; calculate answers; and prepare solutions. Public speaking and/or drama courses will make you a better speaker and a better expert witness. The ability to write clear, understandable reports aimed at nonscientists is a must. Salaries vary across the country and from agency to agency. You will never get rich, but you will have a satisfying, interesting career.

So come with me into this wonderful world called forensic science. You will be intrigued and entertained. These books are awesome!

—Carla M. Noziglia MS, FAAFS

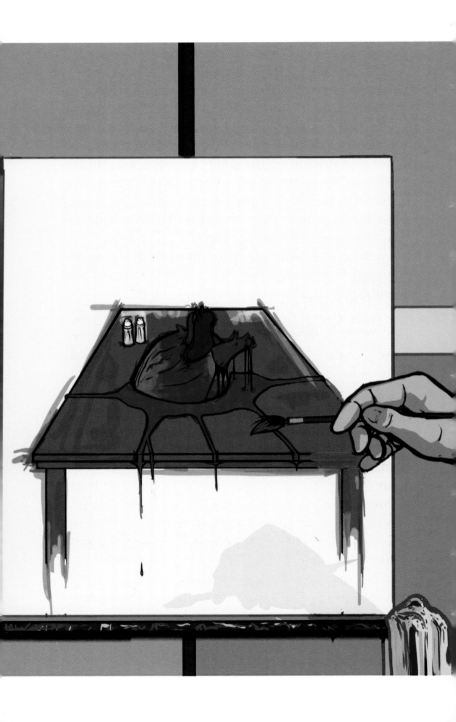

Chapter 1
THE DANCE OF LIFE AND DEATH

The heart lay on a table, looking a little like a skinned chicken, blood oozing from the arteries at its top.

"That's disturbing," said Sarah Crown.

Jessa Carter dabbed some white oil paint into the alizarin crimson on her pallet, then added it to the picture with her brush. "You don't approve of my technique?"

"As a work of art, it's outstanding. I think you've already surpassed my skills. As a reflection of a young lady's soul . . . I'm worried about you, Jessa."

Jessa turned to look at her teacher. Sarah Crown was in her late twenties and already nationally famous for her paintings. She lived with her husband, the millionaire businessman Daniel Crown, in this cabin-styled mansion in the woods, which also doubled as her studio and classroom for private art lessons.

"It's only a painting," Jessa said.

"Paintings like this require more than technique," her teacher replied. "If your soul was not bleeding, you could not have created that."

Jessa twirled one of her long, matted locks with the wooden end of her brush.

"Still thinking about your boyfriend?"

"He's not my boyfriend anymore. He's moved on."

"But you haven't."

Jessa shook her head.

"Maybe time will change things. Lots of relationships break up, come back together again. It takes forgiveness but—"

"No! I know it would be the noble thing, but. . ."

"You can't."

Jessa sighed. "It's hard to trust boys—even without betrayal. I learned as a little girl that men can be. . ." She shook her head, reluctant to say more. "Monsters," she finally bit out, as though the word were something loathsome she could snip to pieces between her teeth.

The older woman's eyes softened. "I'm sorry." She brushed her fingers across Jessa's face. "Poison in the soul can be just as deadly as poison in a person's body."

Jessa's cell phone rang and she flipped it open, relieved to have the moment interrupted. "Hello?" She listened a minute, then said, "I'll be over in about half an hour," and put the phone down.

She turned to her teacher. "There's been a break-in at the Temple. Detective Kwan wants me to help her investigate." Jessa was a member of Crime Scene Club, a unique cooperative effort between her high school and the local police department. The club's teen members had the opportunity to investigate real crimes.

"A break-in at the Temple?" Sarah was clearly astonished. She attended services at the Temple of Universal Truth, as did Jessa's mother. Sarah's husband, Daniel Crown, and Jessa both went to worship there occasionally, and Jessa and Sarah both attended yoga classes at the temple twice a week, as well.

Jessa put away her paintbrushes and hugged Sarah. "Thanks for listening, and . . . caring about me. See you soon."

"It's always a delight spending time with you, Jessa. I know you're carrying a load of hurt, but you're a fine young woman, truly. I expect you'll do great things for the world someday."

As Jessa rolled away on her bicycle she looked back over her shoulder at the Crown house. In many ways, the Crowns' lives seemed so idyllic, with their enormous home and servants. Who could want anything more? And yet there were times when Jessa thought the house seemed unnaturally lonely, creepy.

Her bike picked up speed as it swished down the twisting road past pine trees and aspens. As Jessa headed toward downtown and the scene of the crime, she wondered, *Who would break into the temple—and why?*

Twenty minutes later, she squeezed her brakes and came to an abrupt stop in front of the elegant Asian-looking building on Leroux Street that had once been a private home before its conversion into a center for yoga, meditation, and spiritual enrichment. Now, the sacred space was cordoned off with yellow tape marked Crime Scene: Do Not Enter.

At the door, Detective Dorothy Kwan of the Flag-staff PD greeted her. The thirty-something Asian-American woman was dressed as impeccably as always.

Someone had broken into the temple in the early hours of this morning, Detective Kwan told Jessa. The unknown intruder had shattered the pane of a rear-facing window and entered the building, knocking over a potted plant in the process. The detective handed Jessa a camera and asked her to photograph the site.

The petals on the floor are so lovely . . . fragile, broken. Jessa deftly spun the long lens of the expensive digital camera, bringing the delicate white and yellow flowers into sharp focus. *Click.*

"Hurry up. This is a crime scene, not art class." Wire, the thin boy with the face of a young John Lennon and the brains of a total genius, chided Jessa. He was another member of Crime Scene Club.

"Wire, you should take time to smell the flowers." Jessa grinned at him.

"Jessa, if you're done photographing the point-of-entry, could you come here and help me with something?" Ms. Kwan called from the far end of the room.

Jessa took a few more medium-range shots of the scene, then strode over to where Detective Kwan was talking with a man in a long, East Indian white shirt, black slacks, and sandals. Jessa was familiar with Prakash Jones, priest and founder of the Temple of Universal Truth. Prakash was probably in his forties, but his boyish face and long locks of curly red hair made him look deceptively young; a strict

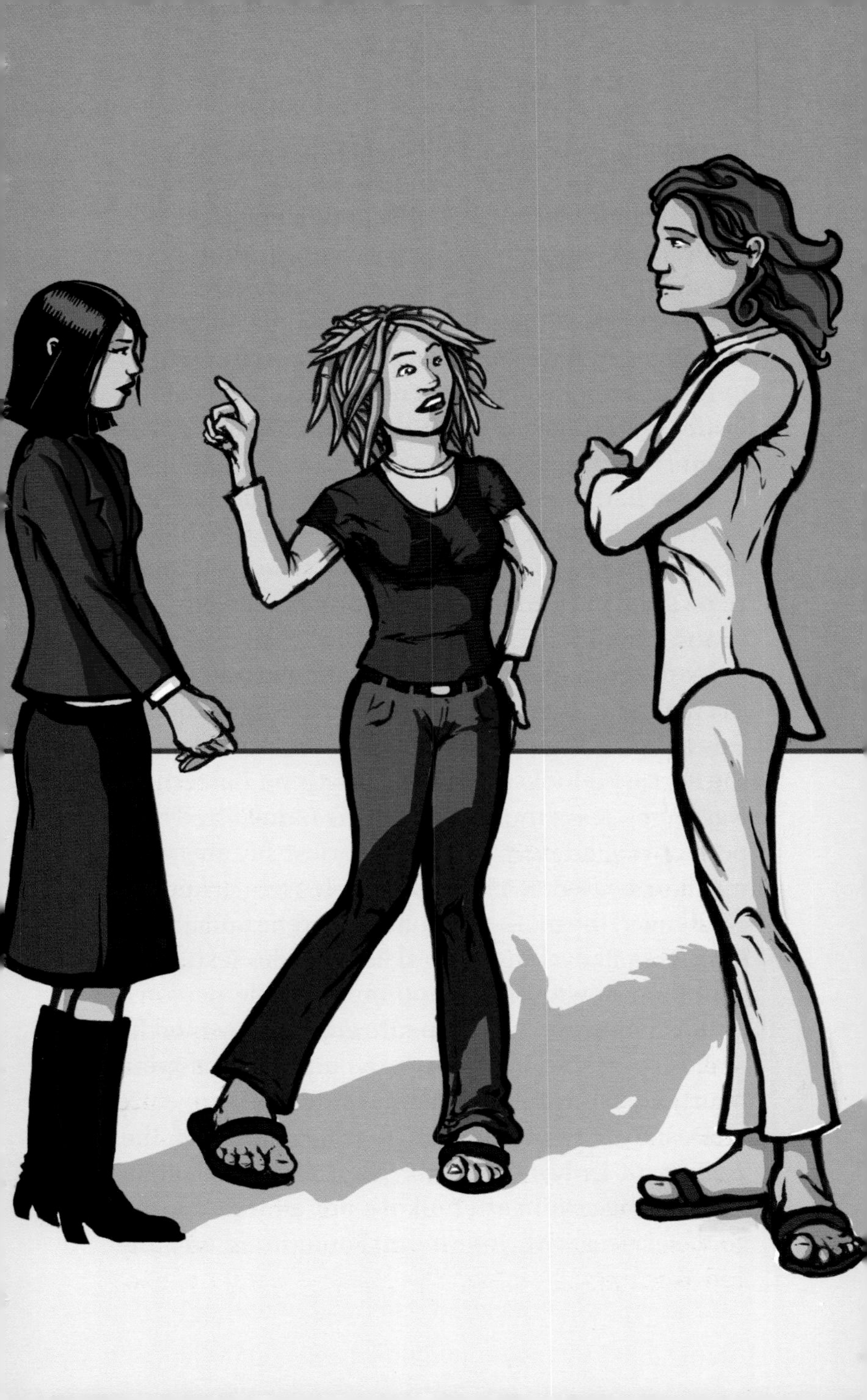

daily regimen of yoga, tai-chi, and jogging coupled with daily doses of herbs and a strictly vegan diet added to his youthful, healthy appearance.

Prakash taught the yoga classes that Jessa attended twice weekly, and he led services at the temple. Prakash also lived in the rooms above the temple's ground-floor sanctuary, though he had unfortunately been out last night, meditating alone in the woods, according to the statement he had given Detective Kwan.

Jessa had heard the story a dozen times of how, searching for enlightenment, this California native had journeyed to Nepal and India, where he spent years studying under various gurus. After returning to the states to teach others what he had learned abroad, Jones changed his first name to Prakash, the Sanskrit word for "light." Some people thought this name change was hokey, but those were mostly the sort who looked down on anything Eastern or New-Agey. Jessa thought Prakash's name fitted him perfectly; she'd never heard the priest say anything mean or heated. Even when people were ornery or challenged the man, he remained serene and unruffled. Jessa had a long mental list of dishonest, arrogant, and downright disappointing male persons; Prakash, however, was the rare guy who seemed as real, respectable, and worthy as one could hope a man—and spiritual teacher—would be.

Despite her admiration for the leader of the Temple of Universal Truth, Jessa only worshiped there on occasion; after all, it's not all that cool to go to services with your mom. Sometimes, on Sundays, she went instead with her friend Aleesha to the Beulah Land Church of Heavenly Salvation, where Reverend Clarise Williams shouted and worked up a sweat while the choir wailed and the Hammond organ swelled up and down in rhythm with the preacher's yells. Jessa wasn't sure what to make of Christianity—she knew it had its dark side—but a Deity who could inspire music like that must be pretty awesome, she thought.

"Priest Jones tells me you are familiar with the statue that was taken from this pedestal," Ms. Kwan said, interrupting Jessa's thoughts.

Jessa nodded. It was an amazing piece of art, one she had often admired.

"Do you think you could draw an accurate picture of the statue from your memory?" Jessa had used her talents on their previous case, when her sketch of a suspect helped police recover a price-less collection of Native art.

"I can try." Jessa made her voice sound modest, but she knew full well she could render a near-perfect likeness. "Prakash, you don't have a photograph?"

"It seemed inappropriate to capture an image of the ineffable with a piece of technology."

Behind her, Jessa heard Wire let out a rude "Humph." She hid a smile and asked the detective, "Do you have a sketch pad handy?"

Dorothy Kwan reached into her crime kit and produced a spiral-ring notebook with blank pages, along with a couple of sharpened pencils. Jessa pulled up a yoga pillow, sat cross-legged, and started to sketch as Prakash leaned over her shoulder, making occasional suggestions.

The Dancing Shiva, also known as Nataraja, is a common theme in Eastern art, but Jessa knew that to most Western minds it is a perplexing combination of moving energy and stillness. The god is portrayed amid a circle of fire, his multiple arms and legs spinning the flaming arc. Shiva's left hand is ablaze, while his right hand holds a drum: symbols of destruction and creation. This particular Nataraja statue was exquisitely carved and overlaid with gold leaf.

Twenty minutes after she began sketching, Jessa looked over her shoulder at Prakash for approval of her drawing.

"Marvelous. You have talent from the gods."

"Thanks, Prakash. I'm grateful for my gifts."

She handed the picture to Detective Kwan, who added some notes about the size and material of the missing statue.

Then Jessa noticed the priest's face; he was looking again at the picture, his brow furrowed. "Is something wrong?"

"Oh, the picture is excellent. I was just thinking . . ."

The detective and Jessa waited for the priest to finish his words. Finally, he said in a grave tone, "Shiva dances to create and to destroy: it is all one. He has been taken from here for a reason. And I wonder—what will he create? What will he destroy? I believe momentous events are about to occur."

May 1

Jessa's Journal

I hate to talk about the past. Is that because I'm ashamed? Because it hurts so much? Or is it the fear of talking to another person, because I'm worried what they will think of me? Sarah is the only one I've said anything to besides Mom and that goofy psychiatrist we visited.

Sarah is so amazing. She lives in that huge, elegant mansion, has servants and all kinds of stuff—but she's still so real, so normal to talk to. I wonder about her private hurts. She doesn't seem to get along well with her husband, Daniel. He's the one with all the money. I know she married him out of love, not greed—but I don't think they're very happy together now. Anyway, my lessons with Sarah are better therapy than that psychiatrist ever was.

Crime Scene Club is good for me, too. Sometimes it's stressful, but most times CSC is a good reason to wake up and pull myself out of bed. I'm especially excited about tomorrow. CSC received an immense grant from state Senator Robbins, as a reward for helping his son on our second case. So tomorrow we have the unveiling of a whole new building on campus—our own professional crime lab, with all sorts of amazing technical stuff inside it.

I wonder—where is the Dancing Shiva statue tonight? I don't see spiritual realities quite the way Prakash does, but I am curious: what changes will that flaming wheel of destiny bring to my life?

Chapter 2
NEW LAB, NEW GIRL

Next morning, Jessa sat in her first period class, World Literature, with Miss Rojas.

"Today we're going over the opening chapters of *On the Road*. What are your impressions of the book so far?"

"Weird," Wire volunteered, "it's all nonsense."

"Where can I meet a guy like Dean Moriarty? I want him," said Maeve Murphy, licking her lips. Maeve is always covered from head to toe in black attire and her head is topped with mop-like dark hair. She's also a member of CSC, and is the club's wild child. Maeve's gothic flair definitely livens up their cases.

"Let's get serious," Miss Rojas pleaded.

Jessa raised her hand.

"Yes?"

"Kerouac breaks the mold of conformity to show us reality in all its tarnished glory. He turns us onto all the beauty in life. This book rocks."

Jessa glanced furtively toward the side of the room where Ken Benally sat. The handsome boy was staring out the window...was he genuinely disinterested or trying to avoid looking at her, she wondered? Ken used to be Jessa's boyfriend, until she caught him kissing another girl. Since then, she barely spoke to the boy, and avoided calling him by name.

"I expect you each have different impressions of our author," Miss Rojas continued. "Kerouac is still unique and divisive, even a half century after he wrote this book. Now I want you to examine his famous quote, '*The only people for me are the mad ones. The ones who are mad to love, mad to talk, mad to be saved.*' Divide into pairs and discuss what that saying meant in Kerouac's life, and then what it means to you personally."

Maeve asked Jessa, "Wanna be my study buddy?"

"Sure."

"Anyone lacking a partner?" Asked Miss Rojas.

Ken reluctantly raised his hand. Jessa flashed a smug grin. *Serves him right.* There was a knock at the door. "Come in," the teacher shouted.

All eyes gazed at the elegant creature who stepped shyly into the room. She was tall, leggy, wearing a short red dress, custom-tailored, and matching pumps. Long silky brunette hair cascaded perfectly off her shoulders.

"I'm a new student...the office said to report here," she said in a little-girl voice.

"Ah, yes. I heard you were coming," Miss Rojas replied. "What's your name, again?"

"Veronika—spelled with a 'k' not a 'c'—Veronika Abazana."

"Welcome to Flag Charter, Veronika."

"Thanks."

"Been in the area long?"

"We've lived in Flag for almost a year now; I was going to the other high school while on the waiting list for this one. And before that, I lived in Long Beach, California."

Jessa noted how the class stared at this newcomer; the girls appeared apprehensive, like animals warily eyeing some new beast in their jungle. The boys, however, were staring with wide eyes and moistened lips.

"Oh my God," one of the boys suddenly shouted, "I saw you on *American Idol.*"

Veronika flashed an "aw shucks" kind of smile and said, "I didn't last long...they only aired one of my songs before I was eliminated."

The excited boy went on, "You sang that *Santa Baby* song. You were...very...ah... talented." Jessa suspected he was going to supply another adjective—something related to male lust fulfillment—but caught himself before it came out.

"Well," Miss Rojas grinned ear to ear. "We're always excited to get fresh talent at Flagstaff Charter, Veronika. Today we are studying *On the Road.* I just asked the class to divide into pairs for an assignment and...wasn't someone lacking a partner?"

Ken raised his hand again. He was smiling now.

I know that smile, Jessa thought. *It's the look he gets when he learns a new riff on guitar, or he solves a mystery or...the way he used to look...at me.*

After school, Mr. Chesterton, the teacher who worked with CSC, ushered the club members into their new building. It was a bungalow, newly built, with the words *Crime Scene Club Forensics Laboratory* painted neatly on the outside. Inside, the room was filled with shining new equipment; row upon row of recently purchased state-of-the art technology.

Wire looked like he had died and gone to heaven, practically drooling over the instruments.

"Nancy Drew never had tools like these," said Lupe, a small, thin Latina. *Lupe is a lot like Nancy Drew*, Jessa thought; she has a sharp mind and she's usually very strait-laced. Except for one time...the time that Jessa caught Ken and Lupe kissing.

Her thoughts were interrupted as Detective Kwan entered the room. "How do you like your new crime lab?" the policewoman asked.

"Pinch me," Wire replied, a blissed-out expression on his face.

"Have a seat and I'll explain what you're looking at," the detective said, grinning. "We may have the best crime analysis facilities in Northern Arizona, right here." She pointed to a trio of large flat screen monitors. "These are all hooked up to the fastest, most powerful desktop computer available."

"Wow," Wire whispered, obviously impressed, "almost as good as the system I have at home."

The detective continued, "We have incubators, mixers, shakers, a centrifuge..."

"Could make great mixed drinks," Maeve chuckled.

"Shut up! We're all underage," Lupe retorted.

Wire continued to salivate.

Ken appeared distracted.

"This lab is equipped with a variety of micro-scopes," detective Kwan continued, obviously enjoying herself, "an automated micro position-ing scope, a biological scope, and a metallurgical scope. There's an array of ultraviolet light tools and an automatic blood sample analyzer," she grinned patting a large, cabinet-like machine. "We also pur-chased—you're not going to believe this—our very own polygraph, or lie detector."

I could have used that not so long ago, Jessa thought, glancing at her ex-boyfriend.

"And to top it off...a state of the art mass spec-trometer," Ms. Kwan indicated what looked to Jessa like a washing machine attached to a chest-high pile of computer towers and a monitor.

"Uh, Ms. Kwan?"

"Yes, Jessa?"

"What is a mass specter...trauma...mater?" *Dang, I try to ask intelligent questions, but somehow they always wind up sounding stupid.*

"I've heard of these," Lupe spoke up. "Basically, this instrument can tell you what anything is made of chemically."

Know it all. "And that's helpful how?" Jessa inquired.

"Do you ever watch CSI on TV?" Lupe asked Jessa.

She nodded.

"When you watch the CSI shows, half the things they do investigating crimes use mass spectrometry," Lupe explained. "This machine is one of the best instruments for forensics."

"Sounds like that could be helpful if someone gets poisoned," Maeve flashed a sinister grin.

"Poisoning...sounds like something out of a Miss Marple mystery," Lupe quipped.

"Not just in novels," Mr. Chesterton, who had been listening quietly to the conversation, jumped in. "Poisoning used to be the artful murderer's weapon-of-choice. Some of history's most famous figures—Socrates, Cleopatra, and Hitler died of poison. Furthermore, there's a huge list of famous people who *might* have been poisoned—including Alexander the Great, Mozart, Napoleon Bonaparte, Charles Darwin and Joseph Stalin. Just think...if mass spectrometry had existed in ages past, we could know for sure if they were poisoned or not."

"On a positive note," Detective Kwan added, "modern forensic science has made a huge dent in the number of poisonings. Like Mr. Chesterton says, poisons used to *be de rigueur* for murders. Nowadays, very few homicides are done that way. In a recent year, only twenty eight out of more than eighteen thousand registered murders in the US were done by poisoning. Thanks to wonderful machines like this"-- she ran her fingers across the front of the mass spectrometer-- "murder by poisoning is hard to get away with."

"But," Wire asked, "isn't it true that more unusual toxins might still go undetected?"

"If any kind of toxin has entered a victim, the MS can find it," Detective Kwan replied. "Problem is, there are so many chemicals in a human body that finding a very unusual toxin is like searching for a molecular needle in a haystack. Not knowing what to look for, you are unlikely to find it. But again, poisoning is out-of-fashion."

"Oh, Mr. C ?" It was the first time Ken had spoken at this meeting.

"Yes?" Chesterton answered.

"I promised that new girl I'd give her a ride home today. She doesn't have a car and doesn't know many kids at our school yet. May I be excused early?"

The teacher nodded, and Ken leaped like a rabbit for the door.

Jessa sucked in her breath. *There's two people I'd sure like to poison about now*, she thought.

Chapter 3
PERIL

An hour later, Jessa was once more working on her painting in Sarah Crown's mansion studio. Japanese flute music from a CD player filled the room. As Jessa painted, she found herself feeling soothed. After about twenty minutes of working silently, she felt calm enough to chat with Sarah. She told her teacher about the new crime lab at school and the new girl.

"She might not be such a bad person," Sarah cautioned. "It doesn't sound like she's coming on to your ex. More like he's just showing a little interest in her."

Jessa wrinkled her nose. "I don't want to talk anymore about boy problems. Can we discuss something else?"

"Sure. Let me brew you some herbal tea. Then we can talk about whatever you like."

"Sarah?" Daniel Crown stuck his head through the doorway, frowning. He was an imposing man at least a decade older than his wife, and he always made Jessa uncomfortable. "Is this going to take much longer?" he asked. "I have important clients coming over and I want the house free to conduct business."

Sarah sucked in a breath. "I know you don't want me interfering in your affairs," she snapped. "We'll be done whenever I decide we're done, and I'm sure Jessa can leave the back way without disturbing your little get-together."

Jessa caught a strange expression in Mr. Crown's eyes before he turned and stalked away. It looked worse than anger. Almost like hate.

"I–I can go now," Jessa offered. "I don't want to cause any trouble between you and your husband."

"Don't be ridiculous. You're my guest," Sarah assured her, but Jessa could see how upset she was.

"Looks like you have your share of men problems," Jessa said in a whisper.

Sarah shrugged. "It hasn't been the marriage I dreamed of. But I try to always see the glass as half full, rather than half empty."

"That sounds like something Prakash would say."

Sarah smiled. "It does. I guess I learned it from him."

Jessa twirled her brush between her fingers. "You hang around the temple more than I do—so is Prakash for real? I mean, it's hard to believe any guy could be as good as he seems."

"I've known Prakash for three years," Sarah replied. "And in that time, I've never seen him lose his temper or speak unkindly of anyone. That's pretty amazing."

"He's one of the most eligible bachelors in Flagstaff. Does he have a girlfriend?"

"Officially, no." Sarah glanced at Jessa, her lips curved in a mysterious smile. "I happen to know he is seeing one of the women at the temple. They have a secret relationship."

"Who is she?"

Sarah shook her head. "I can't tell. They're not free to be together right now. Maybe someday." She sighed.

She looks so sad, Jessa thought. *She must really care about Prakash to be so worried about his relationship with this woman.*

"Sarah!" Mr. Crown's voice echoed up the staircase. "I told you I need room for guests. What do I need to do to make you get that kid out of here?"

Sarah's eyes flashed, but Jessa no longer felt any desire for a cup of herbal tea. "I think this painting is just about done," she told Sarah. "Can I take it home now? I'll be careful not to smudge the paint."

Sarah Crown shook her head. "Why don't you leave the painting here and let it dry? I'd like to look at it more, and maybe come up with some other suggestions by next week. And Jessa? I'm sorry about Daniel's rudeness."

"No problem, Sarah. And thanks again for continuing to teach me. I know you'd make a lot more money working on your own paintings."

"Don't be silly. I enjoy our time together." Sarah Crown got up from her chair and gave Jessa a hug. "I never had a little sister, but if I did, I think she'd look and sound a lot like you."

Jessa loved to hear such affirmation. Sometimes she felt as though Sarah, Prakash, and her mother were the only people in the world who truly knew her—and still appreciated her.

"Same time next week?" Jessa asked before she left.

"For sure," Sarah replied.

As Jessa walked away, she looked back over her shoulder. Sarah was standing now on the upstairs balcony outside her studio. She waved, and Jessa waved back at her mentor. "'Bye!" she called.

From the Crown mansion, Jessa bicycled to the Northern Arizona University Library, stopping en route at a natural food store to pick up something for supper. Then she did her schoolwork at the university library. She knew that some students—like Wire and Lupe—didn't have to study much, and still got excellent grades. Other students, like Maeve, didn't really care about achievement or failure. But Jessa couldn't sail along without effort and she cared about her grades, so she needed to spend substantial time each week in a quiet, study-friendly environment. The university library was the perfect place to find solitude and do her homework.

By 9:30, her brain had absorbed all the algebra and world literature it could hold. She left the library and retrieved her bicycle, switched on the battery-powered headlight and taillight, and pedaled a mile north to her home, a small, red-rock house she shared with her mother and two cats. As she stepped inside, the scent of burning leaves assailed her nostrils.

"Mom, the whole house reeks of pot," she yelled.

"Hey, Jessa, give me a hug. I'm all lonely tonight." Her mother enclosed her in her arms and squeezed.

Jessa pulled away. "I keep telling you, someday you're going to get busted—and then what will happen to me?"

"Jessa, I'm tired. Can't we just be friends?"

Jessa sighed. "Sure, Mom." Sometimes she wondered which one of them was the teenager and which one was the adult. "Mind if I watch the news?"

"What you wanta watch that for? It's always so negative."

"I like to know what's going on in the world."

"My smart daughter, I'm so proud of you." Her mom hugged her again.

Jessa plopped down on the big green couch; the springs were so shot that she sank into the middle almost to the floor. She reached for the TV remote. "Ouch!" she cried as a tiny clawed paw pulled at a lock of her hair. "Stella—bad kitty!" She clicked on the remote, and the KFLG ten o' clock news began.

"A sad day for Flagstaff," the news anchor intoned, "as one of its finest artists passed away this evening."

"*What?*" Jessa jumped to her feet.

The newscaster continued, "Nationally known painter Sarah Crown is reported dead tonight, apparently due to a heart attack at the young age of twenty-eight."

The TV remote fell from Jessa's hand.

A half hour later, Jessa had recovered enough to flip open her cell phone. She spoke a few moments on the phone, her brow furrowed. Then she shut the phone and asked, "Mom, can I borrow the car?"

"Sure dear, but don't stay out too late."

"I'll come back soon as I can. Thanks, Mom." She kissed her mother goodnight and started out the door.

As soon as she left the house, Jessa became aware of the sweet odor clinging to her clothing and hair. Automatically, she pulled a bottle of perfume out of her big leather purse and sprayed her favorite patchouli and honey scent thoroughly over her person. *No point giving Detective Kwan the wrong idea*, she thought wearily, though nothing really seemed to matter much right now. She couldn't believe Sarah was really dead. *No way she had a heart attack. No way.*

Jessa's mind was racing so fast that she pulled up her mother's rusty old station wagon outside the Crown mansion before she was even aware she'd made the trip. A pair of squad cars were parked in the driveway. Jessa knocked, and a policeman opened the door.

"Go away, kid, this isn't a good time to be dropping in."

"But I'm Jessa Carter from Crime Scene Club. Ms. Kwan is expecting me."

The officer gave her a suspicious look.

"It's all right, Officer Parker," a woman's voice came from behind the police officer. "I told Jessa she could come here."

He stepped aside to let Jessa in.

"Oh–oh—" Jessa stared at what was sprawled on the living room floor. She grabbed the back of a chair to keep from falling over. Tears blinded her, and her stomach threatened to lose its contents.

"Oh, Jessa, I should have thought!" Dorothy Kwan took Jessa by the arm and pulled her outside again. "I was forgetting that you've never seen a death scene in person before. Let's step outside a moment. I could use some fresh air."

"Th–th–thanks." Jessa let the detective guide her to a mission-style wooden bench on the wide porch, where she dropped down, feeling as though her legs had turned to noodles. She hugged herself and tried not to cry.

Detective Kwan took a seat beside her. "Sure you're all right?"

Jessa nodded but still couldn't speak.

"There was something important you want to tell me?"

"I was with Sarah—uh, Mrs. Crown—this afternoon. She's my private art instructor."

"Oh Jessa, I'm sorry. No wonder you're so upset. If I'd known she was someone you know, I would have insisted we meet elsewhere. You two were close?"

"Yes."

The detective looked thoughtful. "I know this is painful, Jessa, but maybe you could help me answer some questions. Do you feel up to that?"

Jessa nodded again.

"Okay, thank you." Detective Kwan's eyes narrowed in thought. "Did Mrs. Crown have any health issues that you know of?"

"No way. She eats a strict vegetarian diet, she does . . . I mean, she did yoga three times a week, and she jogs—jogged, I mean—all over the mountain trails."

"She didn't complain of any aches or pains when you were around? Did she get out of breath easily? Ever say that her chest was hurting?"

"No!" Jessa lowered her voice to a whisper. "That's why I'm here, Ms. Kwan. I had to tell you— Sarah was in perfect health, as of a few hours ago. I was just here, with her. She was fine. There's no way she could have had a heart attack."

The detective asked quietly, "You suspect foul play?"

Jessa turned and met Ms. Kwan's eyes. "I do."

"Do you suspect anyone in particular?"

"Her husband." Jessa voice was so soft that the detective had to lean closer to hear her. "He's mean to her. They had a disagreement this afternoon while I was here."

"Did he threaten her?"

"No. But when he looked at her—he looked like he hated her."

Ms. Kwan looked thoughtful. "He seems very broken up tonight, really distraught."

Jessa hesitated. "Could he be putting on an act?" she asked finally. "Have you ever seen people do that? People who were actually guilty?"

Detective Kwan was silent for a long a moment. "Yes," she said at last. "I have. I'll tell the coroner to look at Mrs. Crown's body very carefully. And I'll keep a sharp eye for anything out of place."

Jessa let out a long breath she hadn't realized she'd been holding. This was all she could do for Sarah now, she realized. "Thanks, Ms. Kwan."

The detective put her hand on the girl's shoulder. "I'm sorry for your loss. Believe me, I'll do right by your friend."

Jessa nodded and blinked back fresh tears. Then she got up and headed for her mother's car. Once she was out of sight of the mansion, she parked and leaned her head on the wheel. There was no need to fight her tears any longer.

It was eleven-thirty by the time Jessa got home, but she didn't feel tired yet. She sat in her room, strumming her guitar; Ken and Carlos were the real musicians in their band, but she could do chords and often played the guitar for her private enjoyment. Tonight she sung the mournful words of an old tune: "Fare you well, fare you well, I loved you more than words can tell."

When she was crying too hard to sing any longer, she put down her guitar and pulled her journal out of the drawer by her bed.

Jessa's Journal

May 2

You said I was like your little sister.
I felt the same.
Gentle angel.
Inspired artist.
Truest friend.

Do you still exist, in some other world?
Last Sunday the choir at Beulah Land Church
sang up a storm about "Glory Land."
They made it seem like...
Like the best concert ever in the history of
the world.
Like a non-stop party.
Like happiness.
Like being married to the greatest lover in
the universe.
Is that where you are now?
Are you happy—I mean really happy?
What kinds of incredible landscapes are you
painting tonight?

I know this was no accident.
No sudden failure of health.
How did he take your life?
Did he choke you?
Oh God, that's too awful to think.
Did he poison you?

Sarah, I swear by everything precious
I will not
I will not
I will not forget you
Ever.

And I promise,
I will see justice done for you.
Whatever it takes.

Chapter 4
THE GIRL IN JESSA'S PLACE

The next day, the roots-rock group Red, White, and Blues rehearsed during lunch hour. Jessa was the band's lead singer, but now she avoided the group so she wouldn't have to see their bass guitarist— her ex-boyfriend Ken. To avoid practice, she went for a walk instead in the woods beside the campus, thinking about Sarah, wondering what Detective Kwan might have discovered.

As Jessa made her way back to campus, she heard music: the familiar sounds of the band. But—

Who is that singing my part?

Jessa ran inside the building and looked in the music room's open door. There stood Veronika, crooning vocals into a microphone, nearly licking the metal tube as though it were a lollypop. Jessa leaned against the inside of the door, arms folded, scowling, until the band finished playing.

"What's she doing here?"

"You weren't here for practice, we needed a vocalist, and. . ." Carlos, the group's lead guitarist, let his words trail off. Ken looked down at the ground and didn't say anything.

"I had . . . to go to the doctor," Jessa retorted.

"Every day for the past month?" Carlos looked skeptical.

Jessa shrugged. "She can't do that number—that's my part."

"I don't want to make trouble," Veronika said in her little-girl voice.

"You're not," Sticks, the drummer, assured her.

Jessa put her hands on her hips. "I'm the singer. We don't need another vocalist."

"You can both sing," Ken said. "Veronika practiced with us today so she'll perform with the group. Jessa, you can do back-up vocals, or sing harmony with Veronika."

Jessa felt like a steam kettle ready to whistle. Before the scream could burst from her lips, she turned on her heel and strode away.

Maeve was leaning against a locker in the hallway; she called out to Jessa as she stormed by. "Hey!"

Jessa came to a halt. "What?"

"Wanna get together and push some needles into a doll?"

"Does that really work?"

Maeve grinned. "No, but you'll feel better."

After school, Jessa waited outside the CSC building before the club met. She saw Ken approaching and stepped in front of him.

"We need to talk."

"We do?"

"Isn't it a bit soon for you to go after another girl? And what about Lupe? I thought she was the one you were interested in."

Ken looked uncomfortable. "Who said I'm going after anyone?"

"Don't play stupid with me."

"Veronika's new here. She needs friends at the school. I'm just being friendly."

"Right." Jessa laughed. "You're helping the poor little lonely thing fit into Flag Charter?"

"Yeah, pretty much."

"Bull."

"Besides, Jessa, you said we're both free to date now."

"Yes, but I meant . . . eventually. Not right away."

"It's been six weeks."

Their discussion was interrupted by Mr. Chesterton calling from inside the building, "Time to get started. Important things to talk about today!"

Jessa threw a last glare at her former boyfriend and stomped into the room. Ken followed her, but she noticed he seated himself as far from her as he could.

Ms. Kwan nodded at them. "Unfortunately, we have no new leads on the case of the stolen statue. We've gone over all the documentation from the scene of the theft thoroughly. Whoever did this was a smart one."

Then why did he knock the plant over? Jessa wondered, but before she could say anything, the detective continued speaking, driving all thoughts of the statue from Jessa's mind.

"Meanwhile," Ms. Kwan said, "I've been looking into the sudden death of Mrs. Sarah Crown. I examined the scene of her death very carefully, but found nothing unusual—no signs of struggle or foul play. The coroner also did a thorough examination." Jessa thought Ms. Kwan was talking a more slowly and quietly than she usually did, as though Jessa would be less likely to be upset if the detective lowered her voice.

"Any sign of asphyxiation or poisoning?" Lupe asked.

Detective Kwan shook her head. "Mrs. Crown drank some herbal tea about fifteen minutes before death, according to the coroner. Mr. Crown said that was her usual habit. There was nothing unusual in the coroner's blood tests, and no marks of strangulation or other violence. Officially, she died of a heart attack."

"Can't you check more thoroughly? That herb tea could be a means for poisoning," Jessa urged.

"Yes, I've thought of that. The coroner's report is in. But with Wire's help, I did some more work here today. I've done my best, Jessa."

Jessa sat up straight as Wire walked over to the mass spectrometer. "Detective Kwan was able to borrow this from the coroner." He held up a test tube full of thick red liquid.

"Is that—?" Jessa bit her lip, unable to finish the question.

"Sarah Crown's blood," Wire said matter-of-factly.

Jessa's fingers curled into fists, but she tried to keep her face calm.

"Mr. C let me out of physics class to work on the sample this afternoon. There's a lot of preparation work before this machine can do its thing." Wire pointed to the MS.

"What did you find?" Jessa asked, trying to mask the impatience in her voice.

"I tested for arsenic, strychnine, thallium, amphetamines." Wire folded back his fingers to keep count. "Cyanide and phosphates."

"And your results?" Jessa couldn't keep her voice from rising.

"Nothing."

Jessa sank back in her chair. "Can't you look harder? There are other poisons."

"We could look—if we knew what we're looking for."

"I'm sorry," Detective Kwan said. "This is now a closed case—or more accurately, a case that never opened. We've done a thorough job looking into the details of this unfortunate death, and from everything we can see, Sarah Crown died of a heart attack. It is unusual and tragic when a healthy young person dies that way, yet such things do happen."

"But her husband was mean to her. . . ." Jessa couldn't believe CSC wasn't going to do anything to bring Sarah's killer to justice.

"Half of all married people say they are unhappy with their spouses," Detective Kwan said, her voice gentle. "That doesn't mean they will commit murder."

May 3

Life sucks.
Totally.
He-who-shall-not-be-named is a complete jerk.
Why did I ever care for him?
More mysterious: why do I still care for him?
Lots of reasons. But I don't want to remember those right now.
I want to scream.
Or strangle someone, watching him make googly eyes over that skinny wannabe model.
Why did she ever have to come to Flag Charter?
She's managing to destroy what little happiness is left in my life.

And then, even worse, I have to deal with Sarah's death.
I used to think Ms. Kwan and Mr. Chesterton and all the kids at CSC were so smart, so much more intelligent than I am.
I'm not so sure now.
There is no way Sarah just happened to have a heart attack.
He did it.
I'm certain in my gut.

But how?
There had to be some other sort of poison, something Wire didn't test for.
Radiation maybe? I read somewhere about a former Soviet spy poisoned by a radioactive toxin so deadly and small it could be held in a pinpoint.
Have to ask Detective Kwan to check for that.
I'm not going to let Daniel Crown get away with this.
The PD and CSC can give up on it. Fine.
Let them. Wimps.

I'll see that you get justice, Sarah.
Even if I have to take some risks.
And it looks like I will.

Chapter 5
PRIVATE INVESTIGATION

The next day there was no school in the morning due to a teacher in-service. Carlos left a text message on Jessa's cell: `Band practice. 10AM.`

If they think I'm going to stand and sing next to that American Idol has-been, they better think again, Jessa told herself. Instead, she borrowed her mother's car and drove up the forest road to the Crown mansion. *Time for action.*

A maid answered the door. "Can I help you?"

"I left my painting here." Jessa spoke in her best bimbo voice. "May I get it?"

"Sure." The servant stood back to let her by. "You can find your way to Mrs. Crown's—to the art room?"

"I think I can find it," Jessa replied innocently. "Although sometimes I get confused in this place. It's so big!"

"Call if you need help," the woman told her. "I'll be cleaning up down here."

Fantastic. You do that. Jessa climbed the staircase to the top floor. She peered into the room adjacent

47

to Sarah's studio. At one end was a small altar, with a bronze Buddha and several small bowls filled with now-faded flowers. In front of the altar and bowls was a thick pillow. *Sarah's meditation room.* There didn't seem to be anything suspicious in there, so Jessa moved on. *What am I looking for, exactly?* she wondered.

The next room contained a huge bed, covered with silky red sheets. On a chest beside it were several pictures of Sarah and Daniel Crown, hugging, laughing. *Maybe they got along better than I thought.* They apparently shared one bed, and they looked so happy together in the photographs. *Am I wrong to suspect him?*

Giving up, Jessa went into the art room and took her painting off the easel. She blinked away tears, recalling how just a few days before she and Sarah had shared their thoughts in this very room. She'd never know now what advice Sarah would have given her for the painting. The tears spilled out of Jessa's eyes and rolled down her cheeks.

She went down the stairs and was headed for the door when she heard high-pitched laughter from a side room. Silently, she crept to the doorway and peeked around the corner.

Two people were reclined on a sofa. The man had his back to her, but she was certain it was Daniel Crown. All she could see of the woman was two long, shapely legs and long hair that hung over the arms of the sofa. With careful, cat-like motions, Jessa set her painting on the floor and opened her cell phone.

Not the best camera in the world, but good enough to show the world just how quickly Mr. Daniel Crown has recovered from his wife's terrible death.

Just as Jessa pressed the button on her phone-camera, a woman's voice made her jump. "Hey! What are you doing?"

The next day during the club meeting, Jessa sat listening to Mr. Chesterton, her thoughts wandering.

"Susan Brown murdered her husband by means of anti-freeze in his chocolate cake," Mr. C was saying. "When an autopsy revealed foul play and all the evidence pointed in her direction, she admitted to the killing—but justified her actions because the husband was having an affair with a younger woman. So my question today is—what do you think of Susan Brown? Was she crazy? A deeply disturbed woman who had lost touch with reality? Or an ordinary person who was overcome with jealousy?"

"She had to be crazy," Wire stated. "Her actions were totally illogical. She should have murdered her husband's lover, not her husband."

She should have killed both of them, Jessa thought.

"But people aren't logical," Lupe put in. "We make our decisions based more on feelings than facts."

"True," Mr. Chesterton agreed, "although our emotions might have more reason behind them than you imagine. Take jealousy—the strongest yet most destructive emotion. What causes us to be jealous?"

"Natural selection," said Wire. "People who are jealous are more apt to pass on their genes to the next generation. It's our bodies' way to make sure we win in the struggle to reproduce."

"Wow, you're romantic," Maeve said. "I can just see you using that for a pickup line, 'Hey ladies, wanna win the biological sweepstakes with me?'"

"Evolutionary biologists do agree with Wire," Mr. Chesterton affirmed. "Jealousy—even murderous jealousy—seems to be hardwired into our bodies. In a survey of people around the world, 80 percent of women and 90 percent of men admitted to thinking about murder, even going so far as to imagine in detail how they would do it. And can you guess the number-one reason for fantasies of homicide?"

"Jealousy," Lupe replied.

"That's right. Even more sinister, another study found that half those people said they would actually murder a cheating lover if they were certain they wouldn't get caught."

Ken looked up from the design he'd been doodling on his notebook. "Mr. C and Wire, you're assuming humans are just matter, just bodies and brains full of chemicals. But if people are made of spirit—more than flesh and bone, more than biology—then jealousy isn't some normal, reasonable thing. It's a terrible mistake."

Jessa's eyes narrowed. *I could do some terrible things to Veronika, and I wouldn't feel guilty for an instant.* She pushed aside the ugly thought, realizing that Mr. C's discussion might relate to the death of her teacher and friend. What drove Daniel Crown to kill his wife? If Mr. Chesterton was right, it seemed as though Sarah Crown had had a more likely reason to commit murder than her husband had.

There's a piece missing from this puzzle.

The next day during lunch, Jessa seated herself at a picnic table beside Wire. Lupe soon joined them.

"You get a text message?" Wire asked the girls.

Jessa shrugged. "I haven't checked."

"Ms. Kwan wants us to have a special CSC meeting after school," Lupe said. "She says there are new developments in the case of the stolen statue."

Maeve and her friend Sean joined them at the table while Lupe was speaking. "Darn," Sean said, "that ruins our plans."

Jessa cocked an eyebrow. "Plans?"

"We were going to shop together for our Spring Fling Dance outfits," Maeve explained.

"You going to the dance with anyone?" Sean asked Lupe.

Lupe looked at Wire and smiled.

"You two?" Sean was clearly flabbergasted.

Wire's cheeks turned pink. "It's strictly platonic."

"We're just friends," Lupe declared the same instant. "It's nothing romantic."

"My girlfriend couldn't make it to the dance," Wire added.

"Your girlfriend?" Maeve raised her eyebrows at him.

"What? Geeks can't get girls?" He looked insulted.

"We just didn't know this particular geek had someone special." Sean was obviously curious as well.

"Who is she?" Maeve insisted.

"QTAnimeChick."

"That's a name?" Maeve looked skeptical. "You made that up."

"It's her screen name," Wire replied.

"Ohh, she's an online girlfriend. It all becomes clear now."

"So what's wrong with that? Experts say it's the best way to start a relationship."

"Have you met her?" Maeve wanted to know.

"No, but I have her picture." Wire pulled out his wallet and flipped it open.

Sean whistled. "Not bad!"

Maeve gave him a jab in the ribs. "Cool it."

Lupe peered at the picture, and her forehead wrinkled. "Uh, Wire? QT kinda looks like a girl I saw in *Teen Model* magazine."

"Really? She's a model? She never told me."

"That's not my point. You know sometimes . . . uh, people in online relationships, they're not exactly the same as the pictured . . . oh gee, how can I say this?"

Wire looked uncomfortable and then changed the subject. "So Jessa, you going to Spring Fling?"

Jessa stared at the ground, a lump in her throat. Before she could answer, Sean said, "Have you heard the news?"

She looked up. "What news?"

"Ken asked Veronika to the Spring Fling. Looks like they could be a new item—" He broke off as Maeve gave him another jab with her elbow. "Ow! What'd I say?"

"Excuse me," Jessa whispered. She stood up from the table. "I have to go study."

That afternoon, the members of CSC met in their lab. Jessa glared at Ken across the room. She wished she had supernatural powers, like some imaginary superhero who could reduce the boy to smoldering ashes with her incendiary gaze.

Detective Kwan stood in front of the club with a large cardboard box beside her. She motioned toward it. "The good news on our case is—we found the stolen statue."

"And the bad?" Lupe rose to the bait.

Ms. Kwan opened the top of the box and pulled out a golden arm, then a golden torso, broken in half, and finally, a severed golden head.

Jessa winced. "Oh no."

"Where'd they find it?" Maeve asked.

"In a dumpster, downtown."

"Fingerprints? Tool marks?" Wire inquired.

"No prints. It was probably smashed with a sledgehammer."

"But why?" Jessa felt anger building inside her.

"Someone doesn't appreciate oriental art?" Maeve asked.

"This seems like something deeper than 'doesn't appreciate,'" Mr. Chesterton said. "I'd say this shows extreme anger toward this god—or someone associated with the god."

"A hate crime?" Wire whistled softly. "I never heard of a hate crime toward New-Age types like the people who go to the Temple."

"Anything's possible," replied Mr. C.

"Speaking of anything's possible," Jessa said, "did you check for uranium poisoning in Sarah's—Mrs.

Crown's blood?" She knew she had a one-track mind, but she couldn't help it.

"Results are negative," Detective Kwan replied. "And that's not our case, Jessa. Remember?"

"No sign of any other chemical?" Jessa insisted.

"She died of a heart attack," the detective said. "I know it's sad but it happens. Now we need to get back on track and—"

"Wait a minute," Jessa pleaded. "There's a new twist I haven't told you yet. Look what I saw at the Crown mansion." She pulled several pictures out of her bag and passed them around.

"Wow—paparazzi Jessa!" Maeve exclaimed.

"Yuck!" Wire said. "Were you like being a peeping a tom or something? How'd you get these?"

"Is that Mr. Crown?" Lupe asked.

Jessa nodded. "Uh-huh."

"And the, ah—lady?" Mr. Chesterton wondered.

"No idea."

"What happened next? Did it get more interesting?" Maeve leaned forward and licked her lips.

Lupe scowled at the black-clad girl. "You really are sick."

"The maid caught me taking pictures," Jessa explained. "I had to leave quick."

"Did Mr. Crown see you?"

"Thank God, no. I told the maid I liked the room and wanted a picture of the décor."

Maeve looked disgusted. "That's the worst excuse I've ever heard."

"Did she believe you?" Lupe asked.

"I doubt it. I didn't stick around to find out—I just ran out the door."

Lupe's lips twisted as she looked down at the photo. "I can sure tell Mr. Crown is really broken up over the loss of his wife."

"This doesn't prove anything," Detective Kwan put in finally. "I have to remind you all—Mrs. Crown died of a heart attack."

"What?" Jessa was incensed. "How can you still say that? It proves he didn't love his wife. He's a dirty two-timer!"

"Lots of men cheat on their spouses—and we don't know that he was unfaithful while she was alive."

"But—"

"Jessa, I'm sorry. But this is not evidence of anything."

"Wait a minute," Jessa insisted. "The last time I was with her, Sarah said to Daniel Crown, 'I know you don't want me interfering in your affairs.' I thought 'affairs' meant business, but in light of this—"

Dorothy Kwan shook her head. "Those pictures could certainly be embarrassing for Mr. Crown, but they show nothing illegal, and they're certainly no proof of murder. Furthermore, Jessa, what you did *was* illegal—an invasion of privacy. If word of those pictures ever got out, he could sue. And judging from his reputation, he probably would do just that."

Jessa bit her lip.

I'm trying, Sarah, but everything I do just turns out wrong.

But I'll keep trying.

Chapter 6
IT'S ALWAYS DARKEST JUST BEFORE PITCH BLACK

"Sarah Crown was radiant. An angel. A burning ember. A light warming us, illumining our way, igniting us with her fire."

Prakash's voice quavered, as though his own emotion overcame him. Dressed in a robe of shimmering material that reached to the floor, he spoke without notes, with no holy book in his hands. A hundred-some pairs of eyes watched him, reflecting the flames from small, handheld candles.

Jessa knew that Sarah's body was still in the morgue; Detective Kwan had convinced the coroner to hold off on releasing it to Mr. Crown—just in case. But Prakash had decided to go ahead with the planned memorial service.

Jessa glanced sideways to where Daniel Crown stood, dabbing a handkerchief at his eyes. Jessa saw no moisture on the man's cheeks, though. In fact, she thought—or was it just her imagination—that the wealthy businessman was glaring at Prakash with the same hatred Jessa had seen on his face the afternoon of Sarah's death.

As the priest continued to speak, Jessa heard his voice crack. "As one flame lights another, so the radiance that was Sarah has not gone out. Rather, it has moved on, passed into another form that we can hardly even imagine."

Jessa found it hard to focus on Prakash's words. In her mind's eye, she could see Sarah in yoga class, standing on one foot, arms extended straight outward like a perfectly poised ballerina, frozen in a graceful yet seemingly impossible balance. The next instant, Jessa saw Sarah in the studio; she remembered the gentleness of Sarah's hand on her face. . . .

A life-size photograph of Sarah stood on an easel in the middle of the temple. Prakash gestured toward the picture and invited mourners, "Come. Send your good thoughts to our departed loved one."

Jessa waited her turn in line, then faced her friend's smiling face. *Sarah, if you can hear me, I want you to know—I haven't given up. I'll find out who killed you, I promise. It isn't turning out to be as simple as I thought, but I'll keep on the case. I'll see that you get justice if it's the last thing I do.*

As she moved past the picture, she found herself face to face with Daniel Crown, who was greeting his wife's mourners. He held his hand out stiffly toward Jessa, but she noticed his jaws were clenched. She hid a shudder as she quickly grasped his hand and moved on.

She drifted over to speak with Prakash. "You sounded so sad when you spoke about Sarah," she commented.

He nodded. "I grieve her loss. She was dear to me. And I see from your face that you also grieve."

Jessa nodded. "She was my art teacher—and maybe my closest friend."

"How terrible this must be for you then," the priest said. "Is there someone else you can talk to now that she is gone? Someone who understands your sorrow?"

"No." Jessa looked into his kind eyes and found herself wanting to pour out her heart. "I used to have a steady boyfriend. But he cheated on me. I was a fool to love him." She choked back the tears that threatened to spill out. "I guess I'm a worse fool to love him still."

"No." The priest shook his head. "You are not at all stupid. I sense you have been badly hurt, maybe a long time ago—and yet you risked loving, risked trusting this young man. It is never wrong to follow your heart, even if it leads you to pain." He paused, looked into her eyes. "When I look at you, Jessa Carter, I see a wise soul."

I don't feel very wise. But she hadn't wanted to talk to Prakash about herself. She blurted, "Prakash, do you know anyone in the temple who would have reason to . . . to hurt Sarah?"

Prakash looked startled. "At the temple? Certainly not." His face grew hard and the kindness faded from his eyes; Jessa realized she had never before seen him look so angry. But then he excused himself quietly to put away the sacred objects used in the night's service, and she wondered if she had imagined the rage she'd glimpsed in his eyes.

Jessa glanced at her mom, hoping she and Sunshine were ready to leave, but her mother kept on talking . . . and talking. Finally, Jessa told her mother she would walk home.

"Alone? At night? You can't. Jessa, it's almost ten o'clock."

Jessa rolled her eyes. "I know, Mom. That's why I want to get going. I'll be fine. I'm a big girl."

"Well, be careful." Her mother squeezed her tight. "I might spend the night with Sunshine—to comfort each other." She wiped her wet eyes with the back of her hand.

You mean get stoned together. "Whatever, Mom," Jessa said and headed out into the night.

Her path home took her past South of the Tracks, the club where Red, White, and Blues was performing that evening. She had never before missed a gig with the group, she realized. Well, Veronika probably had taken her place, and no one had even missed her. . . .

As she walked past the club, people were pouring out onto the sidewalk. She couldn't help but overhear their comments:

"That new chick is so hot!"

"I can't wait to hear that band again."

"Didn't they used to have some other girl singing?"

Jessa's fists clenched and she walked faster, but the voices seemed to follow her.

"Yeah, blond chick—kinda fat."

Jessa felt her skin burn.

"What's the new singer's name?"

"Veronika—with a 'k' not a 'c.'"

"Ver-on-i-ka, the girl of my dreams . . ."

Jessa stumbled to a stop, leaning against an empty warehouse, fighting her sobs.

"Hey, girl." Jessa was surprised to feel Maeve's arms come around her shoulders. "It's not the end of the world," Maeve whispered in her ear. "Veronika-with-a-K can't sing half as good as you do."

"Does anyone care what she *sounds* like?" Jessa heard the bitterness in her own voice.

And then she saw Ken. She pulled away from Maeve and went to stand in front of him, her hands on her hips.

"Oh . . . hi, J–Jessa," he stuttered. "We missed you."

"I bet you did. Especially with Veronika there beside you. What's the matter, weren't you happy with her performance?"

Ken looked over Jessa's shoulder, clearly searching for an escape route.

"So where is she?" Jessa taunted.

"She left for the night," Ken muttered.

"What, without her new boyfriend?" Jessa challenged.

"Her—?" Jessa thought she'd never seen Ken look so stupid. "She said she ran into some old friends. They left together in a big fancy limo."

"Cool," Jessa snapped. "Must be nice."

Ken shrugged. "Jessa, I want to say, I'm–I'm really, really sorry. . . I—"

"Yeah, you're sorry, all right. A sorry excuse for a friend." She spun on her heels and headed toward home.

As she strode along, not looking at anyone, someone bumped into her. She caught a glimpse of a long coat and a cowboy hat, a dark face hidden in shadow, and then she felt something angular thrust into her hand. Before she could react, he had walked past her and was gone in the crowd. She spun around, searching the throng that was still pouring out from the club, and then she looked at the parcel in her fingers.

It was a big yellow envelope, the kind used in offices. The outside was unmarked. She tore it open—and gasped when she saw what was inside.

It was a picture of Jessa; she recognized the image from her MySpace site. Across her face, someone had scrawled a big red letter X. On the bottom, in the same red marker, were the words:

Quit snooping—or else!

Back home at last, Jessa dropped down onto the decrepit couch, still staring at the sheet of paper in her hand. *Detective Kwan will probably just say this note doesn't prove anything.* She shook with frustration and exhaustion. *How many bad things can happen in one night?*

Then her cell phone rang. "Hello? Mom? Where are you? What's wrong?"

Jessa listened. "I love you, Mom," she said at last, trying to hide the quaver in her voice. "I'll see you when you get out."

She sank back on the sofa. *Busted! How could she be so stupid?*

Mom and Sunshine, both of them in their forties and they were acting like they were teenagers, get-

ting themselves arrested for smoking dope. Didn't her mother know that Jessa needed her? That sometimes it would be really nice to have a mother that acted like a normal mother?

Jessa's Journal

I'm alone.   So alone.
And it's awful dark.   Cold.
Feels like this night is going to last forever.
Mom's in Jail.
    How can adults be so stupid?

There's my picture on the table with a red X across it.
And there are the other pictures In my head.
Picture from my childhood, but they're not cute and
funny like other people's childhood snapshots.
These are the ones I don't ever look at.
Gotta shove them back.
    Send them away, never let them out.
But now they keep jumping into my mind.
No! Can't look.   No!   I WON'T look.

I'm so alone.
Does it mean I'm crazy if I talk to myself?
But I need to hear a voice, any voice, even if it's my own.
"You were a child then," I tell myself. I'm trying to sound
strong, grown-up, like someone who knows what she's
talking about. "You couldn't stop him. Couldn't fight back.
It's not your fault."

I can't see what I'm writing anymore.
The words are too blurry.
But I'm still talking to myself.
"You were a child then, Jessa.
But you're a woman now.
You're strong. Physically and mentally.
You'll always have those little girl scars Inside.
But now, tonight, you don't have to be the victim.
Fight back."

"No. I can't."   "Yes, you CAN!"

I'm having an argument with myself, like I'm a
freakin' nut case.

"No, I can't."   "Fight back."   "No."
"Fight back. You're a woman now."

And then I see Sarah smiling at me, the way
she was the last time I saw her.
"Fight back," I hear her say. "You're a
woman now."

Chapter 7
POISON

Jessa set aside her journal and pen. She felt like she had just woken up from a dream. Calmly, methodically, she walked over to a dresser, pulled out a black sweater and dark jeans, and began changing her clothes. Then she fished in the back of her closet and pulled out a black stocking cap. After wrestling with her dreadlocks, she managed to shove half of them beneath the cap; the other three long strands she tucked under the back of her sweater. In the bathroom, she found her mother's black eyeliner and smeared it on her cheeks.

Fortunately, Sunshine had given them a ride to the funeral, so Jessa had her mom's car. She took the keys from their place on the counter, went outside, and fired up the old station wagon. In the messy backseat, she spotted a black strap and grabbed her mother's bird-watching binoculars. *Perfect.* She sat a moment in the idling vehicle, staring ahead into the night.

Can I do this?

Fight back. You're a woman now.

She drove up the winding road to the Crown mansion; for the last quarter mile, she turned off the headlights and proceeded slowly, then parked off the road behind a grove of small aspens where the car wouldn't be seen from the house.

Jessa crept on foot to within sight of the enormous house. She touched a button on her wristwatch to illuminate the display: 11:33. She wasn't sure what she was looking for; but knew from crime shows that detectives stake out a house when they believe suspicious activities are taking place. If the cops wouldn't do their job, she would—for as many nights as necessary, until something turned up.

As she crouched behind a large tree thirty feet or so from the house, voices floated toward her through the chilly air. Then she saw Daniel Crown and a woman silhouetted in the lit doorway. They were kissing.

A long, glossy vehicle pulled up quietly and a chauffeur stepped out, then faced discretely away from the house as the man and woman parted. Jessa drew back further into the shadows and waited.

Moments later, she heard the car doors close and it pulled away into the night. She peered around the tree trunk, pulled out her binoculars, and focused on the front of the big house.

The living room faced the front, and the shades of the big window were drawn open, so she had a clear view into the room. A fire burned in the grand mantle facing the window. Jessa saw Daniel Crown walk to the center of the room, then lean over.

What's he doing? She saw him hold up a small box; he opened it and pulled out something thin and long. Jessa squinted into the binoculars. *What is that thing?* Then she saw: a cigar. He walked over to the fire to light the stogie, then sat in a chair, his back to the window. She could just see the back of his head over the chair, and little clouds of smoke wafting up from the cigar.

Snap.

A twig cracked, just a few feet to Jessa's right. Her breath caught in her throat.

A shadowy figure was creeping across the lawn, only a yard away from her. He glided past Jessa and on toward the house, silent as a shadow, apparently unaware of Jessa's presence. Cautiously, she let out her breath.

The dark figure approached the side of the house; she saw him pull a tool out from his belt and cut an electrical line. *He's disabling the alarm!* Then, the wraith-like figure opened a window and swung one leg inside. He disappeared into the side of the house.

Jessa reached for her cell phone, unsure of her next move. Should she call the police? Through the lit window, she saw Daniel Crown stand up. Did he see the black-clad man? No. He was looking the other way, toward the staircase. He walked out of the living room, headed away from the open window, unaware of the intruder in his house.

Jessa slid her phone back in her pants; she would call in a minute, but right now she didn't want to

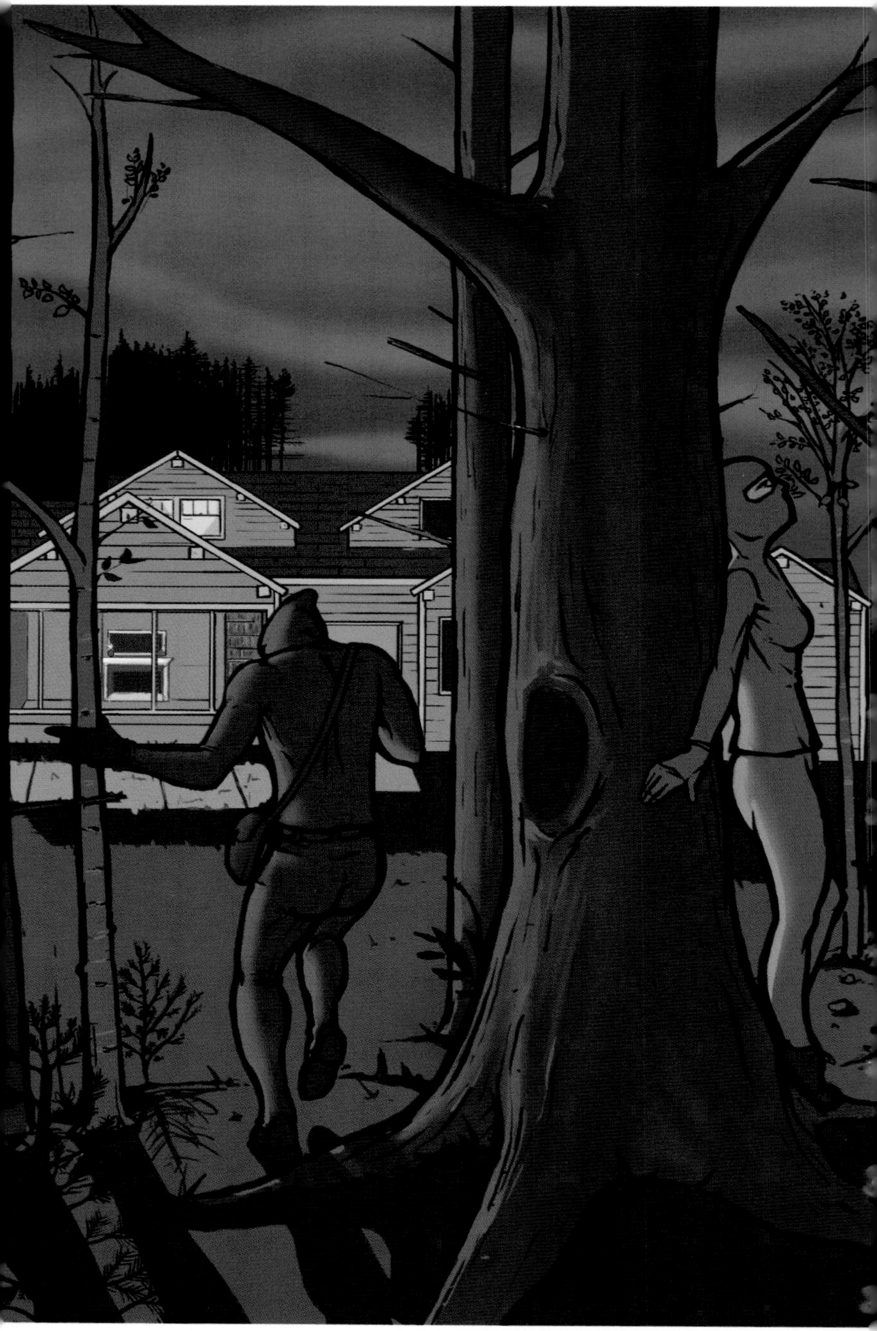

miss anything. She focused the binoculars on the lit room beyond the window.

Daniel Crown was still gone, but the shadow man was creeping into the room. He turned his back to Jessa, then bent down by the fireplace. After a few seconds, he stood and disappeared back the way he had come. Just as Mr. Crown reentered the room, still smoking his cigar, the silent figure slid back out the side window and disappeared into the shadows.

Jessa watched as Mr. Crown stood by the fire for a moment. Then he dropped his cigar and clutched with both hands at his chest. Through the binoculars, Jessa glimpsed his face. She heard nothing but the wind in the trees, but as the muscles of his face contorted, she knew she was watching him scream.

And then he fell forward, disappearing from her view.

Jessa threw caution to the wind as she ran to the window. Inside, Daniel Crown was on the floor, between the coffee table and the fireplace, his face twisted with pain, thrashing like an epileptic having a seizure.

Jessa glanced over her shoulder. The intruder was still out there, somewhere, maybe watching her. Trembling, she flipped open her cell phone, dialed 9-1-1, and reported that Daniel Crown was in need of emergency medical assistance at his mansion.

"Are you giving assistance to the victim?" the woman on the phone asked Jessa.

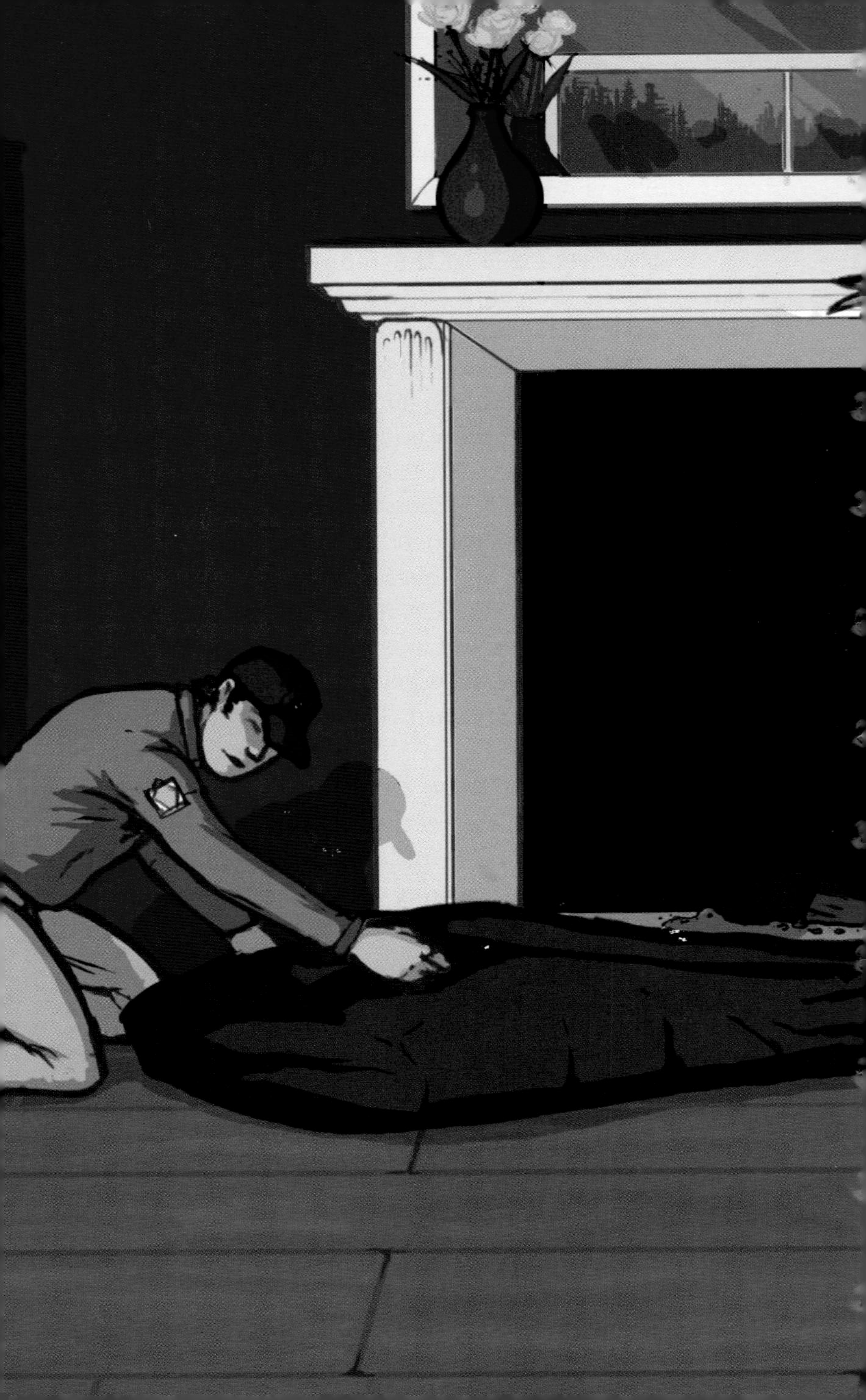

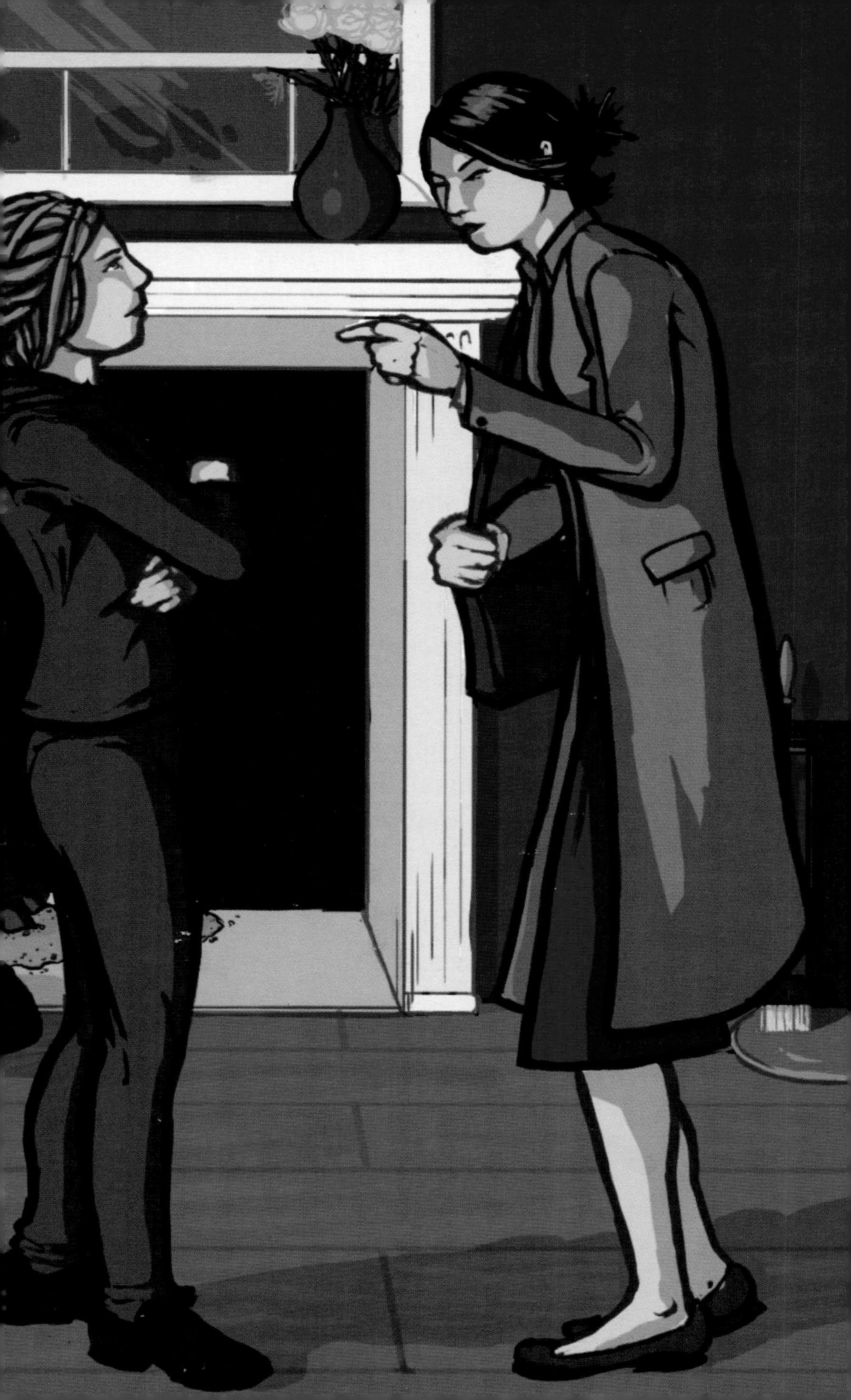

"Just a minute!" She walked around the house to the open window where the intruder had entered; with her free hand, she pulled herself up over the ledge and dropped into the house. Then she dashed through the dark room toward the lamp-lit doorway of the room where Daniel Crown lay twitching on the floor. He looked up at her with glazed eyes, and then he gasped out a girl's name.

"No," she said, leaning over him. "It's Jessa."

The veins in his neck popped, his eyes bulged, his mouth opened and shut like a fish out of water. White foam dribbled out the side of his lips. Frantic, Jessa tried to explain all this over the phone to the emergency operator. At the operator's direction, Jessa tried to take his pulse, but he kept jerking, shaking; he wouldn't stay still long enough for her to feel his heartbeat.

Suddenly, he pushed himself up on one arm. His eyes focused for a moment, bulging with fear as he shouted, "Hell—Hell—Hell Dog." Then he spasmed violently and lay still.

Still as death.

Jessa felt for a pulse. There wasn't any. "He's not moving!" she cried into the phone.

The emergency operator asked, "Do you know how to give CPR?"

"No. I'm not sure what to do." Jessa's breath came and went in small, frantic squeaks.

"Stay calm. We have a team on the way."

Jessa was still crouched beside the dying fire, trembling, when the ambulance arrived. It was too late for them to do anything to help Daniel Crown.

The ambulance crew quickly determined that the death of Daniel Crown was a matter for homicide detectives. "Stay where you are and don't touch anything until the police arrive," they told Jessa.

A few minutes later, Detective Dorothy Kwan arrived, looking unusually disheveled, obviously awakened from her sleep, with three other officers behind her. Ms. Kwan's eyes widened when she walked in and found Jessa, dressed head to toe in black, next to the corpse. "Jessa! What on earth?"

Jessa quickly related the evening's events.

The detective shook her head. "This does not look good. As unfamiliar as I am with teenage clothing trends, I think it's safe to say you are dressed for secrecy. Your prints are on that window and all over the body. You know the victim, and you've stated repeatedly that you blame him for the death of his wife—who happened to be your close friend. That all counts as motive. You're the only one who claims to have seen another 'intruder' tonight, and if he wore gloves, there will be no physical proof of his existence. Like I said, not good."

"Ms. Kwan, don't tell me you think *I* did this?"

The detective leaned close to Jessa, speaking softly in her ear. "I *know you didn't* do this—but I'm seriously worried about what everyone else on the force will think. A basic rule for finding criminals is: 'The first person at the scene of a crime is your most likely suspect.'"

Jessa clutched her arms around her belly. "I don't need any more trouble right now." She curled herself up against the sudden onslaught of pain in her abdomen.

Ms. Kwan touched her arm. "Are you okay? You look like you're in pain."

"I think so. I suddenly had a bad cramp in my gut. I guess it must be my period. But the timing's all wrong."

"Stress can do that."

"Yeah." Jessa wavered, suddenly dizzy. "I feel like I might throw up."

The detective pushed her down onto a chair. "Just rest. But don't touch anything else."

Jessa nodded. Trying to gather her thoughts, she watched as Detective Kwan and her team began taking pictures and notes of the scene. Everything she had assumed about Sarah Crown's death seemed now to be wrong. In light of the evening's events, nothing made sense anymore.

The cramps in her stomach were so bad now that she knew she'd better go to the car and grab a tampon. She stood up, then staggered and caught herself with a hand on the mantle.

"Hey—try not to touch stuff," Ms. Kwan reprimanded. "You're going to contaminate the scene with more of your prints."

But Jessa barely heard her. She hung from the mantle, gasping, her head sagging. As she tried to catch her breath, her gaze fell on a tiny yellow object, stuck in the fireplace grating. The last puzzle piece fell into place in Jessa's mind—and suddenly she saw an image she had never expected to see.

Her head came up. "Ms. Kwan! We have to get to the Temple of Universal Truth—fast!"

The detective hesitated. "Okay," she said finally. "I trust you, Jessa. Officer DeMarco, you come with me and Jessa. You two, stay here and keep reporters and anyone else out of this scene until we get back."

Jessa gave her a shaky smile, grateful for her confidence. As the squad car raced through the streets, sirens flashing, Jessa quickly explained her new insight into the case.

"You're brilliant, Jessa!" Ms. Kwan said. " But we don't have a warrant to enter the temple."

"It's usually unlocked, and I take classes there— that would be excuse enough for me to go in and look around. Right?"

"But anything we find will be no good legally," Officer DeMarco protested.

When they arrived at the temple, the entrance was open, the room inside lit. A paper taped was scrawled with a single word: **Enter**.

As Jessa stared at the paper, it seemed to blur, then rotate slowly. She took big gulps of air, and the note steadied.

"Jessa?" the detective asked.

"I'm okay."

Officer DeMarco looked at the sign and shrugged. "Can't hurt to go inside and see what we see."

"I'll take that note as the owner's permission," Detective Kwan agreed.

Jessa followed the police officers into the room. Before she could take more than a couple of steps, though, she fell onto the polished bamboo floor, gasping in pain.

Detective Kwan knelt beside her. "What is it?"

Jessa couldn't answer. These aches were not menstrual cramps, she realized, at least not like any she had ever felt before. Her face contorted in agony as a giant hammer seemed to drive nails of pain through belly. She clasped her fingers over her mouth, felt the moisture that bubbled there, and remembered the way Daniel Crown had looked before he died. "Poison!" she choked. She clutched at Ms. Kwan's sleeve, knowing she would be dead in a few minutes, just like Daniel Crown had been.

The detective didn't waste a second. "This is Detective Kwan requesting emergency assistance—immediately!" she yelled into her radio, then gave the temple's address.

Jessa screamed as her entire body convulsed with pain. "I don't want—" she moaned.

Detective Kwan leaned closer.

"I don't want it to end this way."

"Detective?" Dimly, Jessa could hear Officer DeMarco trying to get Dorothy Kwan's attention.

"Not now!"

"But, Detective—"

"I said, DeMarco—not now!"

Jessa could feel her heart racing, then slowing almost to a stop. She looked up into Ms. Kwan's face, saw the tears streaming down the detective's face.

"Where are those medics?" the detective snapped.

"You need to see this!" the other officer shouted. "It might save her life."

Jessa managed to turn her head and see that he held a small glass bottle and a piece of paper. With her eyes blurring in and out of focus, she managed to read the words.

Jessa, I knew you'd lead the police here. This is the antidote—in case you were exposed to the toxin. Like I said, you truly are a wise soul. Namaste to you.
Prakash.

Jessa reached a shaking hand toward the bottle. "G–g–give me. . ."

Dorothy Kwan's face was white with tension. "Jessa, he just killed a man—how can we trust him? We can't risk this. We have to wait for the ambulance."

Another spasm wracked Jessa's body. She heard Detective Kwan sob. "Don't die Jessa, don't die. Hang on! Help's coming."

After a moment, Jessa regained control of her limbs and reached out her hand. "Trust him!" she rasped.

"For God's sake, Dorothy, give her the antidote!" DeMarco begged.

Detective Kwan stared at the vial in her unsteady hands. "This better work!" She quickly unscrewed the bottle top and poured the liquid down Jessa's throat.

Jessa's Journal   May 6

I hear about people who have these wonderful near-death experiences: shining light, floating away from the body, seeing lost loved ones, all that. Didn't happen to me. Not even close. Just horrible pain in my gut, muscles that still ache, and memories of agony. It's hell being poisoned.

The doctor says I should rest the next few days, but I think that's what they tell everyone who goes through a traumatic experience, just so the doctor's butt is covered in case I fall at home or something. So I'm lying here, listening to MP3 files and watching videos.

Mom's doting all over me. After an old family friend bailed her out of jail, she came home and dumped all her stash in the toilet. She says she's "turning over a new leaf." Ha, ha. She's done this like a dozen times before. Still, one can hope.

A couple of reporters called. One even left me a note with his number and some questions, "For whenever you feel well enough to answer them." How considerate of him.

I'm looking at the questions now, and one of them asks, "What mental processes did you use to solve this mystery?" I'll bet this reporter plays chess a lot, or reads Sherlock Holmes. Still, it is a good question. But it wasn't really a process—more like getting hit by lightning.

It was the petals. They were stuck in the fireplace grate at the Crown mansion. Those petals—lovely, fragile, broken flowers—exactly the same as the ones on the floor when the temple got broken into. The instant I saw them, everything clicked into place. The break-in at the temple wasn't really about the statue. That was just a diversion. The plant by the window—that was the reason someone broke into the temple. Maybe he knocked it over by accident, perhaps trying to get pieces of the roots.

I guessed all this at the Crown place, but I couldn't prove my guess until talking to Mom later. Prakash often spoke about that plant with his disciples. He would quote the Friar from Romeo and Juliet:

"Within the infant rind of this small flower
Poison hath residence and medicine power."

Prakash used that plant as an illustration that nothing
is good or evil in itself, only in the use of a thing
does it become good or bad. In fact, those little white
and yellow petals make glycerin pills that save the
lives of heart attack victims—and they also make
terribly lethal poison that can stop hearts from
beating.

Daniel Crown hated the temple, but he went
with Sarah on occasion, just to keep her from
nagging. That's what Mom says. Daniel was there one
time when Prakash explained the plant. So he knew
where he could get deadly, hard-to-trace poison,
right here in town.

Why did he kill his wife? Maybe because he
was jealous of her and Prakash; he couldn't stand
to think his wife was truly happy in the arms of
another man. They hid their affair well, but he must
have guessed, the way I did. But I think he killed
Sarah for another reason: because she knew about
his affair with an underage girl. Technically, it was
a case of statutory rape. He could have lost his
reputation, faced legal charges.

So he killed Sarah with a little bit of that
lovely flower, ground up in one of those herbal teas
that she loved to drink. Poor, poor Sarah. And her
murderous husband would have gotten away with it.
The poison wouldn't show up in toxicology tests if
the investigator didn't know what to look for.

But one person knew.

One person saw through it all and realized the
significance of that plant, caught the connection
between the break-in at the temple, the fallen
flower, and Sarah's surprising heart attack.

Why didn't Prakash go to the police with this
knowledge? I may never know. Maybe he didn't
trust them to prosecute the case. Maybe he
feared that Daniel would escape; with all his
money, he probably had a getaway plan in place.

But my best guess is this: Prakash believes in Karma. "What goes around comes around," I've often heard him say in yoga class. This time, he decided to be destiny's payback for his lover's death.

And he planned the perfect revenge killing. No one would ever have cracked that case if I hadn't been watching from the shadows. Prakash sneaked in and dropped petals in the fire. I looked it up on the Internet. That plant is so nasty, even dropping leaves or petals into a burning fire will create deadly fumes. So Daniel Crown walked into his own living room and inhaled a breath of tainted air. And then I walked in, while the fumes still filled the room. My muscles continue to ache, and I'm coughing some. That stuff is murder! (Literally.)

It's called Eranthis, and it grows wild in India. Prakash must have brought some seeds home with him from his travels. The poison is named after Cerberus, the three-headed hound that guards the door to Hades. That's why Daniel Crown's last words were "Hell Dog"—he knew what had killed him.

Chapter 8
BAD NEWS, GOOD NEWS

"Jessa guessed right," Detective Kwan affirmed at the CSC meeting two days later. "All her speculations about the case are verified by scientific means."

"The poison?" Maeve asked.

Wire answered, "I ran blood samples from both Mr. and Mrs. Crown through the mass spectrometer, looking for traces of the glycoside cerberin. Found it in both victims."

"Traces of what?" Lupe asked.

"The active ingredients in that flower from the temple," Mr. Chesterton clarified. "Each victim's blood contained enough toxin to cause death."

"Jessa's pursuit of this case was absolutely brilliant," Ms. Kwan added. "I've worked with some fine detectives, but few have had displayed the clear thinking, tenacity, and courage that Jessa did on this case."

Jessa felt as though her insides were glowing like ET's.

"Can we prove that Mr. Crown killed his wife?" Lupe wanted to know. "How do we know Prakash didn't commit both murders?"

"We searched the mansion," Detective Kwan replied. "Daniel Crown wasn't very careful about things—probably never imagined we'd get a warrant—and he left ground-up pieces of eranthis root in a pestle in his basement workshop."

"So, the murder of Sarah Crown is a closed case," Maeve pronounced.

"It is."

"What about the murder of Daniel Crown? We still have a suspect at large," Wire pointed out.

"An agent at the Mexican border reported someone that looks like Prakash passing through, the morning after the murder," Ms. Kwan said.

"Did the agent stop him?"

"Nope. We didn't have a bulletin out yet."

"So—he's in Mexico?" Jessa asked.

"I don't think so. There were a bunch of new books about travel in Nepal at Prakash's place. My guess is—he's far away from this continent."

Jessa didn't want to say it, but she was relieved. Yes, Prakash had almost killed her—but totally by accident. She didn't really want to see him behind bars. In her mind, Jessa imagined a tall, red-haired man with a backpack and hiking staff, climbing a snowy, high-altitude trail to a remote monastery. Prakash had always dreamed of living in a place like that, though not under these circumstances. She wondered if he'd be able to make peace with the death that he now carried on his conscious—or if he would be haunted by guilt for the rest of his life.

"Unless there are further developments with our fled suspect—and I'm not holding my breath—

the case of the stolen idol, the murdered wife, and the murdered husband are a wrap," Mr. Chesterton concluded.

"What's next?" Wire asked.

Jessa noticed the teacher and detective exchange glances.

"Mr. C? Ms. Kwan? Is something wrong?"

"Well," Mr. Chesterton said, "as the old cliché puts it: we have good news—and we have bad news."

"Always bad first," Maeve said.

"All right." The detective took a breath. "We aren't doing any more field cases."

"What?"

"But that's the whole point of crime scene club."

"I know you're disappointed," Ms. Kwan continued, "but it's too much of a liability to have you teens on the field doing crime work."

"But we're *good*," Lupe wailed. "We've solved four crimes in half a year—we're an important help to the city."

"You kids aren't just good," Mr. Chesterton affirmed, "you're phenomenal. A fact noted by local, state, and national law enforcement."

Some thanks we get for our great detective work, Jessa thought.

"So how can they do this?" Wire asked.

Detective Kwan looked glum. "I'm sworn to protect and to serve—not just the broader community but you five young people as well. I care deeply about all of you. I'll probably never have children of my own so. . . well, I guess I've started to think of each one of you as very special. It's been awful seeing you hurt. Lupe, you took a bullet from the biggest handgun I've ever seen. Maeve, I could hardly hold myself together when you were injured in that car crash. Then Ken, you got your head cracked by that thug in the woods. And just a few days ago, Jessa—well, that was the worst ten minutes of my life, holding you, thinking you were dying. And you would be dead—make no mistake—if the priest had not left that note and medicine." She shook her head. "I know you're all disappointed, but I can't stand to see any more of you hurt."

"I won't get hurt, I'm too smart," Wire stated.

"Humble, too," Maeve rejoined.

"But what will we do with this lab?" Lupe moaned. "You said yourself, it's practically the best crime lab in Northern Arizona."

"We'll still do lab work. We'll meet, and we'll talk about cases. We just won't be involved as directly as before."

"Any chance of reversing this?" Ken asked quietly. "If we stay out of trouble a few months, maybe you and the department will reconsider?"

"Maybe."

I sure hope so, Jessa thought.

There were a few moments of silence, then Maeve said in a fake cheerful voice, "And the good news is?"

"Oh, yes, almost forgot." Mr. Chesterton tried to sound upbeat. "Since we have plenty of extra funding, CSC is paying for all its members to go on a field trip this summer."

"Where to?" Jessa wanted to know.

"Los Angeles. We'll tour famous crime sites, visit with the LAPD forensics crew, and see the popular vacation spots."

"Disneyland?" Lupe asked hopefully.

"The beach?" Jessa added.

"Can we see the LA morgue?" Maeve's voice was eager.

"Hey, QTAnimeChick lives in LA—you can all meet her." Wire seemed unusually excited.

Jessa and Lupe exchanged worried glances. *I sure hope Wire doesn't get his feelings crushed.*

"Hey," Maeve whispered just loud enough so her fellow students—but not the adults—could hear her, "I'll bet we can come up with some pretty cool crime cases in LA. Whether they're official or not."

Jessa was unlocking her bicycle after the meeting when a tall, familiar shadow fell across her. Without looking up, she said, "Want something, Benally?"

"Please, could you call me Ken again?"

She tried not to show emotion, but her voice softened a little. "What do you want?"

"To share a thought."

She straightened and faced him. "Like?"

"You know how the Grateful Dead got their name?"

"Of course. From an old folk tale about dead souls who reward the living, because the living protect their memories."

"Well, I think Sarah Crown must be truly grateful for what you did for her, Jessa."

"Thanks . . . Ken. I appreciate you saying that." She squared her shoulders. "So where's your new girlfriend?"

"She was never my girlfriend, just a way to . . . not think about you."

"You're speaking of her in the past tense."

"She didn't come to school yesterday or today. Miss Rojas said this morning that Veronika moved out of state."

"That quick?"

"Weird, huh?"

Their eyes locked. "Ken, there's something you should know. I wasn't going to tell you—except, now that Veronika's gone. . ."

"Yeah?"

"The night I entered the mansion and Mr. Crown was dying, he saw me, but his eyes must have been blurred by the poison. He called me . . . a name. He thought I was—Veronika."

Ken looked sick as he absorbed the implications of what she'd said.

"You must have suspected," Jessa said quietly. "That limo after the concert . . ."

Ken shook his head. "I guess you never really know a person."

"Yeah, well. . ." She tried to bite back the bitter words but failed; she had recovered from the poison in her body, but she knew there was still poison in her soul. "Now you know how I felt."

"Jessa?" He took a step closer to her. The gentleness in his eyes made her want to cry. "I'd do anything in the world to rewind the clock, to undo that mistake, to not have hurt you."

"Really?" She struggled to hold back the tears.

He nodded. "I'd like to try and start over again, but slowly . . . real slowly. Maybe we could go bowling or go to a coffee shop."

"Thanks. But . . . I'm sorry. I'm not ready for that. Maybe sometime soon, but not yet."

"I understand. I don't blame you."

They stood awkwardly for a few moments. Jessa found she was thinking about the statue of Shiva that had been broken into pieces by Daniel Crown. Shiva, the god who both created and destroyed, had obviously been hard at work in her life. She wondered if in the end, where the balance would lie: destruction—or creation?

Ken put the tip of one finger against her face, a touch so slight she barely felt it. "I promise, Jessa, I swear by my ancestors—I'll never do anything to hurt you again."

"You'd better not, Ken Benally—because I'd kill you if you did."

"Poison?"

She laughed. "You'd never know what hit you."

FORENSIC NOTES

CRIME SCENE CLUB, CASE #4

CHAPTER 1

Evidence List

Vocab Words

alizarin crimson
idyllic
cordoned
regimen
gurus
ineffable
Western
momentous

Deciphering the Evidence

When Jessa uses *alizarin crimson* in her painting, she's adding a paint that contains a deep, rosy red pigment.

Jessa thinks that at least on the surface, the Crowns' life appears to be *idyllic*—carefree, charming, and simple.

The temple is *cordoned* off with yellow police tape, meaning that it is roped off to prevent anyone from entering.

Prakash Jones follows a healthy daily *regimen*: a regulated course, as of diet, exercise, or manner of living, intended to preserve or restore health or to attain some result.

POLICE LINE DO NOT CROSS

1.1 The scene of a crime is secured by the first police officers to arrive. The familiar yellow crime scene tape is placed around the crime scene to stop unauthorized people from entering and contaminating the investigation area.

Prakash studied under Indian *gurus*, Hindu spiritual teachers.

When Prakash refers to the *ineffable* as being something that is appropriate to photograph, he is speaking of a spiritual and sacred quality that is too deep to be expressed.

Jessa is aware that most *Western* minds—people who have grown up in the Americas or Europe—have a hard time understanding the spiritual symbolism of Eastern art.

Prakash senses that *momentous* events are about to unfold; in other words, he believes that something with great and far-reaching consequences will happen.

The World of Forensics

Our English word "forensic" comes from the Latin word forensis, which means "forum"—the public area where in the days of ancient Rome a person charged with a crime presented his case. Both the person accused of the crime and the accuser would give speeches presenting their sides of the story. The person with the best forensic skills usually won the case.

In the modern world, "forensics" has come to mean the various procedures, many of them scientific in nature, used to answer questions of interest to the legal system—usually, to solve a crime. Detective Kwan and the new members of the CSC

1.2 The Forum was the center of political, social, and economic activity in Ancient Rome. Beside housing the courts and functioning as an arena for justice, the area of the Forum included a marketplace, the Roman Senate, and many temples, such as the temple of Saturn, shown here.

will use many of these procedures in their cases. In this case, their fourth, the procedures involved with forensic toxicology will prove to be particularly useful to them.

Toxicology is the study of the adverse effects of chemical and physical agents on living organisms. These substances could be drugs, poisons, or various chemicals that occur naturally in the environment. Toxicology is often considered to be the oldest of the forensic sciences.

Other Forensic Procedures Used in CSC Case #4

Forensic Photography

Using photographs to document evidence is important for many types of cases, including accident reconstruction. The photographs can be used to simply record the surrounding conditions and evidence at the time of the crime—but they can also be taken back to the lab, where computers are used to enhance details on the photographs that might not otherwise be discernable to the human eye.

Recent advances in digital imaging have greatly improved many aspects of forensic photography. Digital techniques allow detectives and the lab technicians who help them to capture, edit, output, and transfer images faster than they could with processed film. In the old days, when photographers depended on darkrooms, many techniques had to be applied through time-consuming trial and error; now, with digital photography, these techniques can be instantly applied on a computer, and the results are immediately visible on the monitor.

Besides the advantages of speed and efficiency, digital photography also offers some techniques that were never available using traditional photography. One forensic photography technique, for example, is the ability to correct the perspective of an image. As long as the photograph contains a scale of reference, it is possible to take an image that was shot at an incorrect angle and correct it so that the scale is the same across the plane of focus.

CHAPTER 2

Evidence List

Vocab Words

conformity
tarnished
divisive
incubators
centrifuge
toxins

Deciphering the Evidence

Author Jack Kerouac was not afraid to
"break the mold of *conformity*"—in other
words, he didn't feel he had to make his
actions match society's expectations.

Jessa speaks of reality's "*tarnished* glory";
she's speaking rather poetically here,
implying that reality is like silver that has
become dull or dirty.

When the English teacher says that
Kerouac was a "*divisive*" author, she means
that his ideas caused disagreements.

The new crime lab has *incubators* and
a *centrifuge*; these are apparatuses in
which environmental conditions, such as
temperature and humidity, can be controlled,

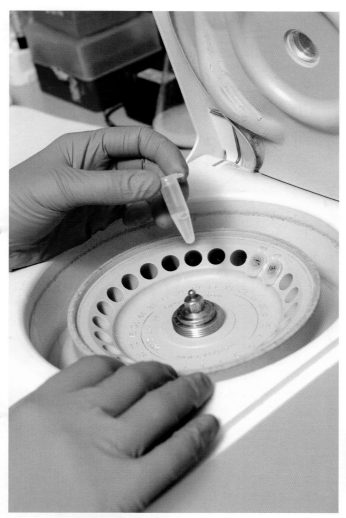

2.1 A centrifuge, like the one pictured here, is used to separate substances of different densities. Small vials are placed in the centrifuge to spin around a fixed axis. The centripetal force causes particles of heavier densities to fall to the bottom of the tube.

providing suitable conditions for a chemical or biological reaction—and an apparatus that rotates at high speed and by centrifugal force separates substances of different densities.

When Wires speaks of *toxins* that may go undetected, he's referring to poisons.

Forensic Toxicology

The History of Poison

Why was poisoning such a popular method to commit murder for so many centuries? Because, for one thing, poisons were readily available: almost any natural substance in the right dose can be poisonous. What's more, many poisons cause symptoms that appear to be common medical diseases, which often lead friends and family (and even physicians) to believe a victim died of natural causes. Arsenic, known as the "poison of poisons," was the most common poison. It was sometimes called the "inheritance powder," since many impatient heirs used it to do away with their elderly relatives.

In the early 1700s, Dr. Hermann Boerhaave may have been the first true toxicologist; he was the first person to use a chemical method for the detecting of poisons, though his method was fairly simply: he placed substances he suspected of containing poison on red-hot coals,

2.2 Hermann Boerhaave was not only an early toxicologist, but also an important Dutch physician and botanist. He maintained extensive botanical gardens at his home; some of these plants may have been involved in his toxicology testing.

and then used the odors that resulted to help him determine what chemicals were present.

Other Forensic Procedures Used in CSC Case #4

Lab Equipment

The "magic" of forensic science depends on state-of-the-art lab equipment. Special microscopes allow technicians to analyze materials that may yield important clues. A micro-positioning scope, for example, allows tiny samples to be exactly positioned in order to be scanned by a probe; a biological scope is a basic microscope that allows semi-transparent samples on slides to be examined with a light shining through them; and a metallurgical scope is used to examine small opaque objects, such as metal samples. Ultraviolet lights are used in forensic labs to reveal marks and substances that would not otherwise be visible to the human eye. It is especially useful for detecting the presence of body fluids.

Mass Spectrometry

How does a mass spectrometer work? First, a small amount of the unknown material is dissolved and injected by needle into a hollow tube. A flow of inert gas (helium or nitrogen, which don't react readily with many chemicals) propels the heated mixture through the coiled glass tube, where a sensitive, computerized detector

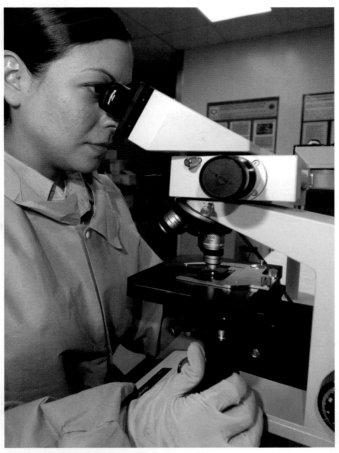

2.3 Forensic science "magic" depends not only on state of the art lab equipment, but also on highly trained lab technicians and scientists who know how to do the work and how to use complex machines like this microscope. Despite what it may look like on television, the real forensic stars are simply lab-based chemists, molecular biologists, or anthropologists who are hired on a case-by-case basis by law enforcement; they are not out on the street fighting crime.

identifies the separate elements at the other end. Each element can be identified by how quickly it reaches the "finish line" (because each element moves at its own speed). An MS can be used to identify many things, including drugs and explosives, as well as poisons. It's also used for blood alcohol evaluations.

The spectrometer can identify the smallest traces of individual chemicals. It does this by bombarding the sample substance with electrons from a heated cathode, which breaks down the sample's chemicals into electrically charged fragments. A magnetic field pushes the fragments into a circular path, the radius of which varies according to the mass

2.4 In many cases, analysis with a mass spectrometer is combined with analysis in a gas chromatograph. The two machines combined are able to identify substances to a much finer degree than either machine operating alone.

Mass Spectrometer

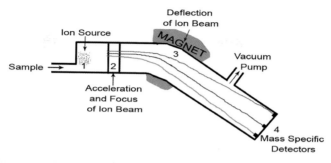

2.5 This figure illustrates the four steps involved in analyzing the masses of different isotopes in a gaseous sample. 1) The sample is converted to charged ions. 2) The ions are concentrated into a beam and accelerated past a powerful magnetic field, which 3) deflects the ion beam and separates it into ion beams of different masses. 4) The different masses are detected and analyzed.

of the fragment. As the magnetic field is increased, a detector linked to a computer records the energy spectrums. The position of each fragment on the spectrum measures its mass, and its intensity indicates its proportion in the sample. A printed readout supplies this information.

Who's Who Among the Poisoned

Socrates

This ancient Greek philosopher was condemned to death and was made to drink a beverage made from the hemlock plant, which contains a neurotoxin that paralyzes the muscles. Although the effects are temporary, without artificial respiration, the victim will die from lack of oxygen, since his respiratory muscles will also be paralyzed.

Cleopatra

The great Egyptian queen is said to have died as a result of the poison from a snake.

Hitler

When the German leader responsible for the deaths of thousands of people during the Holocaust learned that Germany had been defeated by the Allies, he killed himself by biting into a poisonous cyanide capsule.

Alexander the Great

When this great military commander of the fourth century fell ill after drinking too much, he may have tried to regain his health by taking hellebore. Unfortunately, although this plant was a medicinal in small quantities, in larger quantities it can cause cardiac arrest.

Mozart

No one is sure exactly why the musician died when he was only thirty-five. There are many theories, from flu to kidney disease; one theory claims he died of mercury poisoning.

Napoleon

Officially, the French emperor died of stomach cancer, but in 2001, French forensic scientists announced that they had analyzed hair samples from the emperor—which revealed he had died from arsenic poisoning. Historians hypothesize that he may have been killed by undercover British agents.

Joseph Stalin

The Russian dictator was said to have died of cerebral hemorrhage brought on by ill health—but in 2005, the Kremlin revealed that he was most likely poisoned by one of enemies with warfarin, a powerful chemical that thins the blood and makes the victim more apt to suffer a stroke (cerebral hemorrhage). Warfarin is often used to control rat populations.

CHAPTER 3

Evidence List

Vocab Words

affirmation
coroner

Deciphering the Evidence

Sarah's *affirmation* of Jessa means a lot to Jessa, because her words make Jessa feel more sure of who she is; they give her a firm belief in her own integrity and worth.

Detective Kwan plans to tell the *coroner* to examine Sarah Crown's body carefully. The coroner is an officer of a county or city whose job is to investigate not clearly resulting from natural causes.

Forensic Toxicology

The first murder trial to feature toxicological testimony from medical experts occurred in England in 1751. The accused, Mary Blandy, had agreed to marry Captain William Cranstoun; unfortunately, he already had a wife in Scotland. Understandably, Mary's father did not look with favor on the captain as a possible suitor for his daughter—but Mary was in love, and she continued to meet with Cranstoun secretly.

Meanwhile, the captain was deeply in debt. He gave Mary a powder he'd obtained from an herbalist and told her to put it in her father's food in small doses, with the assurance that it would help her become eligible for her inheritance sooner.

3.1 Mary Blandy was hanged in 1752 for poisoning her father with arsenic. This picture shows her while in prison; she is wearing leg irons to keep her from escaping.

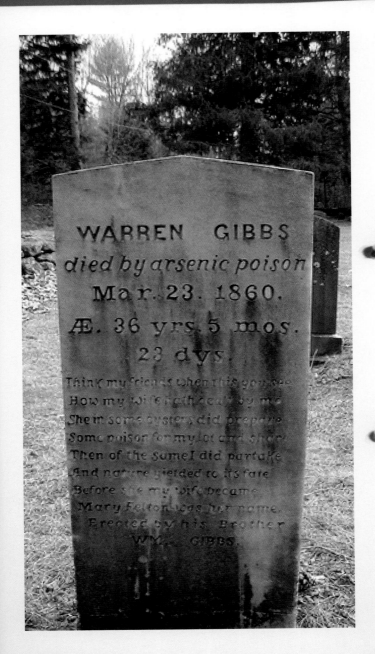

WARREN GIBBS
died by arsenic poison
Mar. 23. 1860.
Æ. 36 yrs. 5 mos.
23 dys.

Think my friends when this you see
How my wife hath dealt by me
She in some oysters did prepare
Some poison for my lot and share
Then of the same I did partake
And nature yielded to its fate
Before she my wife became
Mary Felton was her name.
Erected by his Brother
WM. GIBBS.

Mr. Blandy grew ill. His servant found the white powder Mary had been giving him, and became suspicious of Mary. Blandy, however, continued to trust his daughter; he ate and drank whatever she gave him. Before long, he died.

When the authorities came to arrest them, Cranstoun fled to Europe, but Mary was caught on her way out of town. Four doctors autopsied Blandy's organs and determined that he had been consuming arsenic. The jury found Mary guilty of murdering her father and sentenced her to death.

Today's forensic toxicologists use far more sophisticated methods for determining the presence of poison in the body than the doctors did who testified against Mary Blandy—but the principles are still the same. The presence or absence of a substance in a body can lead to a conviction.

3.2 Arsenic used to be a common method of poisoning. This man, William Gibbs, was supposedly killed by his wife; the poem on his grave reads, "Think my friends when this you see/ How my wife hath dealt by me/ She in some oysters did prepare/ Some poison for my lot and share/ Then of the same I did partake/ And nature yielded to its fate/ Before she my wife became/ Mary Falton was her name. Erected by his Brother WM. GIBBS."

CHAPTER 4

Evidence List

Vocab Words

asphyxiation
strychnine
thallium
amphetamines
cyanide
phosphates

Deciphering the Evidence

Lupe wonders if the coroner found any signs of *asphyxiation* on Sarah Crown's body; these would indicate that Sarah had been killed by an act of choking or smothering.

Strychnine, thallium, amphetamines, cyanide, and phosphates can all be poisonous substances. *Strychnine* comes from the seed of an Indian tree that's related to the nightshade family; it stimulates the central nervous system in smaller quantities and is used as a rat poison in larger concentrations. *Thallium* is a soft, highly toxic metallic element that's used in rat and ant poison. *Amphetamines* are chemicals that stimulate the central nervous system; they're used both medically and illegally (as recreational drugs), but in too high doses, they can cause death. *Cyanide* is an extremely poisonous salt. *Phosphates* are salts used in fertilizer and some detergents; they are harmless and even beneficial in small quantities, but poisonous at higher concentrations.

4.1 Strychnine occurs naturally and used to be used regularly, both as a stimulant and as a laxative. Now, however, people have realized that this substance can be deadly, even in very small amounts.

Forensic Toxicology Case File

Woman Hater

Most people are familiar with Jack the Ripper, but not many people have heard of Thomas Neill Cream, who lived (and murdered) at the same time in London. Though Thomas Neill Cream targeted the same group of victims as Jack the Ripper, prostitutes, he had a very different modus operandi. Cream was a doctor who had been sent to jail once for murdering the husband of a patient with strychnine-laced pills. Once released, he sought vengeance on all women by picking up prostitutes and then giving them pills. He apparently told them the pills were to help prevent sexually transmitted diseases.

Cream eventually was caught and convicted via a combination of arrogance, early forensics and witness testimony. He couldn't resist

More About Forensic Toxicology

Sometimes forensic toxicologists determine whether a person has been poisoned by analyzing a blood sample, as Wire does in this chapter. The coroner may also detect the presence of poison by testing the contents of the deceased person's stomach talking about the cases and one of his friends, a detective, was surprised by the specific details Dr. Cream knew, including the names of two victims that even the police had not known. When bodies were exhumed, they were autopsied and found to contain strychnine, known to be Cream's poison of choice. Finally, one of the women he attempted to kill, Louisa Harris, never swallowed his pills, and so remained alive to testify against him in court.

He was found guilty and hanged on November 16, 1892. One final strange twist is Cream's last words. Some say that he shouted, "I am Jack" as he went through the trap door, but to this day, no one knows what he meant. Some people argue Cream was confessing his identity as Jack the Ripper, but most disagree because Jack the Ripper had a very different MO and was still active while Cream was in prison.

(as the coroner did with Sarah's body). Poison can also be identified by testing urine or even a strand of hair. Other times, however, a full autopsy is required, in which tissue samples are removed from various organs. A living person may be tested for a suspected substance with a basic kit that is a little like the breathalyzer used for detecting alcohol levels. If a quick test like this registers a positive result or if symptoms show something different, a more sophisticated analysis may be required.

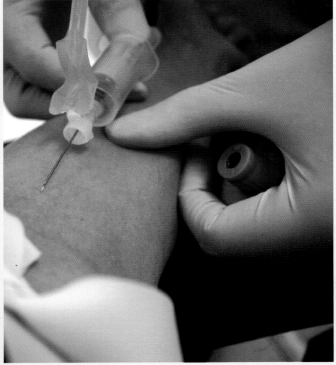

4.2 When testing for drugs with a blood sample, blood is taken from an artery, not a vein. This is because the blood in arteries has oxygen and other gases in it that have not yet been used up by the tissues in the body, making it possible to determine exactly what chemicals are present.

CHAPTER 5

Evidence List

Vocab Words

platonic
evolutionary
incendiary
paparazzi

Deciphering the Evidence

When Mr. Chesterton says that *evolutionary* biologists agree that jealousy is part of physical makeup, he's speaking of scientists who study changes in the gene pool of a population from generation to generation by such processes as mutation, natural selection, and genetic drift.

When Wire and Lupe insist that their relationship is *platonic*, they mean it's free from sexual or romantic attraction.

Jessa wishes she could make Ken *burst into flame* with her incendiary gaze.

Maeve says that when Jessa took Daniel Crown's picture with his unidentified girlfriend, she was acting like the *paparazzi*—photographers who take pictures of celebrities without asking permission.

Forensic Toxicology Case File

Umbrella Assassin

Georgi Markov was a Bulgarian writer who had constantly spoken out against his country's communist government during the Cold War, protesting again and again until he was forced into exile in Britain. One day in September 1978, he was walking to work when he felt an abrupt, sharp pain in his leg. He turned around to see a man picking up an umbrella from the sidewalk pavement, and before he could say anything, the man apologized and then jumped into a waiting taxicab and sped away. Markov went on to work, where he noticed an ongoing pain in his thigh, and a small red, pimple-like bump on his leg.

A day later, Markov was running a high fever. Three days later, he died. In the time between his admittance to the hospital and his death, he was able to speak with his doctors about the experiences described above, and the theory rapidly developed that he had in fact been poisoned. An autopsy of his body ordered by Scotland Yard found a tiny little metal pellet buried in his leg.

Markov's symptoms, particularly the high fever, were consistent with ricin poisoning, and tests of the interior of the pellet revealed that it had in fact held ricin. Ricin is a highly toxic substance made from the shells of castor beans, and intelligence reports from the CIA and MI6 had indicated that the Soviet Union was examining its applications for biowarfare. Indeed, after the end of the Cold War, it was revealed that the Bulgarian Secret Service had assassinated Markov by firing the pellet into his thigh with a CO_2 powered gun hidden in the umbrella.

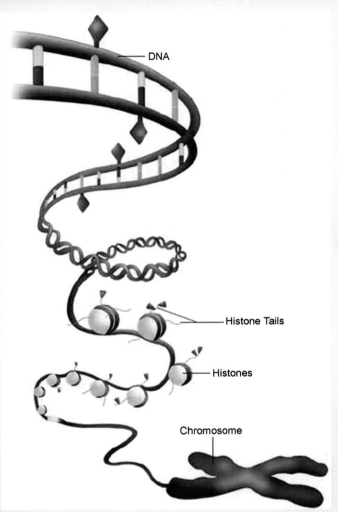

DNA

Histone Tails

Histones

Chromosome

5.1 Mr. Chesterton and the CSC discuss genetics and the evolutionary advantage of jealousy, but genes are even more complicated than they realize. This diagram shows that events and behaviors (such as jealousy) that shape who people are, can control DNA to some extent without actually altering the basic genetic code that gets passed onto the next generation.

Other Forensic Techniques Used in CSC Case #4

Fingerprints

On the surfaces of the hands and feet are tiny raised wrinkles called friction ridges. These ridges are formed while a fetus is still developing within the uterus. Each person's friction ridges are unique; even identical twins do not have the same

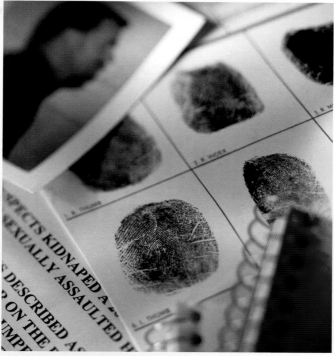

5.2 While everyone's fingerprints are slightly different, there are a few shapes, such as arches, loops, and whorls common to many prints.

fingerprints. What's more, barring scarring or injury, friction ridges remain unchanged throughout life.

When friction ridges come in contact with a surface that is receptive to a print, any material on the ridges—such as perspiration, body oils, ink, or grease—can be transferred to the surface. As you move through life, your fingers (and toes, if you're barefoot) leave telltale marks behind.

Before today's era of computers, manual fingerprint classification systems were used to categorize fingerprints based on general ridge formations (such as the presence or absence of circular patterns in various fingers). In the Henry system of classification, there are three basic fingerprint patterns: arch, loop, and whorl. Each of these also have subcategories. As you can imagine, identifying a suspect's fingerprints was a tedious and enormously time-consuming process. Today, however, computers make this process almost instantaneous—and new and better fingerprinting methods are being developed.

Fast Fact

The first known use of fingerprinting was in fourteenth-century Persia, where government officials used their fingerprint much in the same way we use signatures today.

Tool Marks

A tool mark is a cut, gouge, or scratch caused by a tool coming into contact with another object. These marks are often found at burglary scenes where a building was forcibly entered, but they may also be found in homicide cases where an axe or knife strikes bone. The marks are usually caused by a tool cutting or sliding against a surface that is softer than the tool.

Similar to a fingerprint, tools such as pry bars, chisels, axes, and knives leave behind telltale marks that can be used to identify a particular tool. Tool marks examinations compare a tool mark or the cast of a tool mark against marks produced in the laboratory by a suspected tool. The known and unknown marks may also be compared microscopically.

5.3 Like a fingerprint, each tool leaves its own, unique mark. Forensic technicians can match

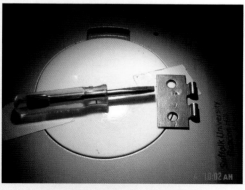

these marks to the tools they came from; in this case, this screwdriver was found to have made the scratches on the door hinge.

CHAPTER 6

Evidence List

Vocab Words

sacred
angular

Deciphering the Evidence

After Sarah Crown's memorial service,
Prakash puts away the *sacred* objects he
used during the ceremony—the items he
considers holy, connecting humans to spiritual
reality.

The object thrust into Jessa hands is
angular, with sharp corners.

The History of Poison

Poison has been around a long, long
time—for more than 4,500 years, ever
since the Sumerians worshipped a goddess
of poisons. The ancient Egyptians also
understood poisons, and in India, around
2,500 years ago, physicians wrote down
directions for recognizing the personality
traits of poisoners. Around 2,200 years
ago, the Greek physician Nicander of
Colophon compiled the earliest known list
of antidotes for poisons.

Our word "toxicology" comes from a Greek word, toxicon, which referred to poison arrows. The ancient Greeks also used hemlock, a poisonous plant, to administer capital punishment. By the eighth century, an enterprising Arab chemist had turned arsenic into

6.1 Gula was the Sumerian goddess of healing, and the patron goddess of physicians. She was also called upon to curse bad people with her poisonous potions. Also called Bau, Ninisina, or Nintinugga, she was depicted with the head of a dog, or alternatively with a dog like this by her side.

125

Médicinal - Toxique
Conium maculatum L
Grande cigüe
Europe Idont Fr.). Afrique du Nord
Anatolie à O. Himalaya, O. Sibérie   Apiaceae

6.2 In Ancient Greece the poisonous hemlock plant was used as a form of capital punishment. The philosopher Socrates is perhaps the most famous prisoner to be executed in this manner.

an odorless, tasteless powder that was impossible to trace in the body until centuries later; this made arsenic the ideal poison for committing murder.

During the Renaissance, poisoners became even more creative. They hid their venom inside poison rings, on swords and knives, in letters, and even in lipstick. Poisoning "clubs" began to meet, and businessmen began poison-for-hire companies.

In modern times, however, forensic toxicology has put an end to such wickedness. Thank goodness!

CHAPTER 7

Evidence List

Vocab Words

methodically
wraith
epileptic
disheveled
contaminate

Deciphering the Evidence

When Jessa gets dressed *methodically*, she's doing it in a slow, deliberate, and careful way.

Jessa sees someone who looks like a wraith—a ghost—enter the Crowns' house.

As Daniel Crown is dying, he looks as though he's having an *epileptic* seizure. Epilepsy is a disorder that has to do with nervous system abnormalities that cause convulsions (or fits) and loss of consciousness.

Ms. Kwan looks *disheveled*—messy, unkempt—because she just woke up.

Detective Kwan warns Jessa not to *contaminate* the scene of the crime: make it impure by introducing substances not originally found there such as hairs, dirt, or fibers—or by disturbing what was originally there.

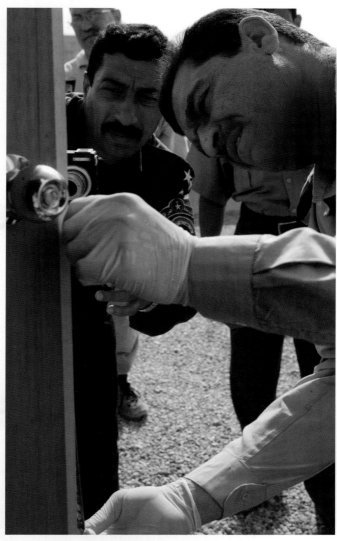

7.1 Police officers and investigators are careful not to contaminate any part of a crime scene. The officers shown here wear latex gloves while measuring tool marks on a doorway.

7.2 Documenting evidence, such as shoe prints found at a crime scene, is only one part of identifying a suspect. Determining the person who had the motive, the ability and the opportunity to commit the crime will all be necessary in order to gain a conviction.

Other Forensic Procedures Used in CSC Case #4

Establishing a Motive

Determining who has a motive—a reason—to commit a crime helps detectives identify likely suspects. Motive alone is not proof, but when combined with "means" (the ability) and the "opportunity" to commit a crime, it can lead to a jury conviction.

Obtaining a Warrant

In the United States (as well as in many other countries, including Canada and the United Kingdom), certain citizen rights are legally protected. In the United States, these rights are guaranteed by the Constitution and the Bill of Rights. A warrant, however, allows police to cross these legal lines.

A warrant is an authorization written by an officer of the court (usually a judge), which commands an otherwise illegal act that would violate individual rights; it grants the person who carries out the warrant protection from any legal damages. The most common warrants are search warrants (which give the police permission to search someone's private property when there is reason to believe that evidence connected to a crime will be found there), arrest warrants (when police bring a suspect into custody until a court officer determines what happens next),

7.3 Police officers typically require an arrest warrant to bring the suspect of a crime into custody. However, there are situations, such as a driving under the influence arrest in which a written arrest warrant is not necessary.

and execution warrants (when a convicted person receives a death sentence).

A typical arrest warrant in the United States, such as Lieutenant Standish is discussing in this chapter, would be worded something like this:

This Court orders the Sheriff or Constable to find the named person, wherever he or she may be found, and deliver said person to the custody of the Court.

CHAPTER 8

Evidence List

Vocab Words

speculation
verified
active ingredients
tenacity
liability

Deciphering the Evidence

Detective Kwan says that all Jessa's
speculations—her guesses—were correct.
She knows this because they were
verified—proven to be true—with scientific
evidence.

When Mr. Chesterton refers to the *active
ingredients* in the plants, he's referring to
the chemicals that cause a reaction in the
body.

Ms. Kwan praises Jessa's *tenacity*—her
ability to stick with what she set out to.

Daniel Crown left traces of the cerberas
plant in a *pestle*—a bowl-shaped container

for pounding or crushing substances with a mortar.

The Flagstaff police department is no longer willing to allow the teens' to be involved in crime cases because of the potential *liability* to the department. In other words, should one of the kids be seriously hurt, the police could have the legal obligation to pay for all damages.

8.1 The Cerberus poison, also called aconite, used by Prakash is real poison that can be made from *Eranthis*, which is a genus of yellow or white flowering plants found in southern Europe and Asia. According to Greek mythology the plants were said to have originally sprouted from drops of poisonous saliva that fell from the mouth of Cerberus, the three-headed dog.

8.2 Many plants are either dangerous or medicinal depending on how they are used. The poisonous plants of the *Digitalis* genus are commonly called foxgloves, and may be grown in gardens as ornamental blooms. An extract from the common *Digitalis purpurea*, shown here, was used as early as 1785 for the treatment of heart conditions.

Wrapping Up CSC Case #4

The CSC has once again solved a crime—and they've also once again proven that crime solving is a dangerous activity. What's more, as in real life, not every question has been answered. In the world of forensic science, everything cannot always be explained, and loose ends often remain to tantalize the detectives. In this case, for instance, who was the man who thrust the anonymous message into Jessa's hands after the concert, warning her to stop investigating Sarah's death? Was it Daniel Crown? Could it have been Prakash? What do you think?

FURTHER READING

Fenton, John Joseph. *Forensic Toxicology. In Forensic Science: An Introduction to Scientific and Investigative Techniques.* Edited by Stuart H. James and Jon J. Nordby. Boca Raton: FL: CRC Press, 2003.

Ferllini, Roxana. *Silent Witness. How Forensic Anthropology is Used to Solve the World's Toughest Crimes.* Buffalo, NY: Firefly Books, 2002.

Howe, Robert F. *Deadly Dose.* Reader's Digest. April 2003.

Innes, Brian. 2006. *Forensic Science.* Philadelphia, PA: Mason Crest Publishers.

Middleberg, Robert. F*orensic Toxicology in the Fore.* Forensic Magazine http://www.forensicmag.com/articles.asp?pid=210, 2008

Trestrail, John Harris. *Criminal Poisoning.* Totowa, NJ: Humana Press, 2000.

FOR MORE INFORMATION

All About Forensic Science. Forensic Toxicology. http://www.all-about-forensic-science.com/forensic-toxicology.html

American Academy of Forensic Sciences. www.aafs.org

Crime Library, "Mass Poisoning" by Katherine Ramsland http://www.trutv.com/library/crime/criminal_mind/forensics/toxicology/index.html

How Stuff Works, "How Crime Scene Investigation Works, www.howstuffworks.com/csi.htm

The Science of Forensic Toxicology. http://www.soft-tox.org/default.aspx?pn=Introduction&sp=Introduction

BIBLIOGRAPHY

Fenton, John Joseph. "Forensic Toxicology," in *Forensic Science: An Introduction to Scientific and Investigative Techniques.* Edited by Stuart H. James and Jon J. Nordby. Boca Raton, Fla.: CRC Press, 2003.

Howe, Robert F. "Deadly Dose," *Reader's Digest.* April 2003.

Midkiff, Charles. "Dated Methods of Poisoning," *Scientific Sleuthing Review.* Fall 2002.

Owen, David. *Hidden Evidence.* Buffalo, N.Y.: Firefly Books, 2000.

Platt, Richard. T*he Ultimate Guide to Forensic Science.* London: DK Publishing, 2003.

Schechter, Harold. *The Poisonous Life of a Female Serial Killer.* New York: Pocket Books, 2003.

Starrs, James E. "Modern Methods of Poisoning," *Scientific Sleuthing Review,* Spring 2002.

Trestrail, John Harris. *Criminal Poisoning.* Totowa, N.J.: Humana Press, 2000.

Wecht, Cyril. *Mortal Evidence.* New York: Prometheus Books, 2003.

INDEX

PICTURE CREDITS

Creative Commons .Attribution .Share Alike (CC-A-SA)
Bauer, Stefan: p. 95
pizzodisevo: p. 134
Qfamily: p 110

CT Department of Public Safety; pg 120

GNU Free Documentation license, Version 1.2
Polimerek: p. 104
Raul654: p. 133

istockphotos.com
Benavidez, Charles: p. 128
tillsonburg: p. 93
Wei Ming, Tan: p. 114
Young, Lisa F.: p. 130

Jupiter Images: p. 99

Miller, Malinda: p. 105

National Institute of General Medical Sciences: p. 117

United States Marine Corps
Maggard, Cpl. Seth: p. 127

United States Navy
McGinley, Ryan: p. 103

To the best knowledge of the publisher, all images not specifically credited are in the public domain. If any image has been inadvertently uncredited, please notify Harding House Publishing Service, Vestal, New York 13850, so that credit can be given in future printings.

BIOGRAPHIES

Author

Kenneth McIntosh is a freelance writer and college instructor who lives in beautiful Flagstaff, Arizona (while CSC is fictional, Flagstaff is definitely real). He has enjoyed crime fiction—from Sherlock Holmes to CSI and Bones—and is thankful for the opportunity to create his own detective stories. Now, if he could only find his car keys . . .

Ken would like to thank the following people:
Tom Oliver, who invented the title 'Crime Scene Club' on a tram en route to the Getty Museum, and cooked up the best plots while we sat at his Tiki bar . . . Mr. Levin's Creative Writing students at the Flagstaff Arts and Leadership Academy, *who vetted the books . . . Rob and Jenny Mullen and Victor Viera, my Writer's Group, who shared their lives and invaluable insights . . . My recently deceased father, Dr. A Vern McIntosh, who taught me when I was a child to love written words. This series could not have happened without all of you.*

Series Consultant

Carla Miller Noziglia is Senior Forensic Advisor, Tanzania, East Africa, for the U.S. Department of Justice, International Criminal Investigative Training Assistant Program. A Fellow of the American Academy of Forensic Sciences her work has earned her many honors and commendations, including Distinguished Fellow from the American Academy of Forensic Sciences (2003) and the Paul L. Kirk Award from the American Academy of Forensic Sciences Criminalistics Section. Ms. Noziglia's publications include *The Real Crime Lab* (coeditor, 2005), *So You Want to be a Forensic Scientist* (coeditor 2003), and contributions to *Drug Facilitated Sexual Assault* (2001), *Convicted by Juries, Exonerated by Science: Case Studies in the Use of DNA* (1996), and the *Journal of Police Science* (1989).

Illustrator

Justin Miller first discovered art while growing up in Gorham, ME. He developed an interest in the intersection between science and art at the University of New Hampshire while studying studio art and archaeology. He applies both degrees in his job at the Public Archaeology Facility at Binghamton University. He also enjoys playing soccer, hiking, and following English Premier League football.